the Gun from Dooley's Desk

7-22-18

To Sandy

Enjoy my storytelling in print. A time gone by.

J Rex Sims

the Gun from Dooley's Desk

J. Rex Sims

Copyright © 2018 by J. Rex Sims
All rights reserved.

First Edition: June 2018

Edited by Raven Dodd, Preserving the Author's Voice
www.ravendodd.com

Cover Design by Len Eckert, iconDoInc.com

Author photograph by Lifetouch, www.lifetouch.com

This is a fictional story. The characters, their names and businesses; locations, episodes, and occurrences are used in a fictitious manner or are the result of the author's imagination. Any similarity or resemblance to actual individuals, living or dead, and current or historical events is purely coincidental.

ISBN-13: 978-1719486453
ISBN-10: 171948645X

Dedication

For my Rotary friend Dave Shellenbarger who gave me the gentle nudge and encouragement to complete my story.

Thanks, Dave. You are the greatest!

Acknowledgements

To my wife Peggy, for sharing the lifetime experiences that are part of this book.

To my editor Raven Dodd, Preserving the Author's Voice, for blending my rambling stories into a cohesive book for your enjoyment, an event requiring all her skills and experience.

To my Rotary friend Len Eckert, iconDo, Inc., for creating the book cover that portrays the content of the story I want to tell.

From the pages of the Wabash Daily News:

Wabash, June 1911

One of the most startling sensations Wabash has had for a long time was the leaving of a baby on the front steps of the residence of Mr. Garl Coleman. The little waif has been since that time carefully cared for by Mr. and Mrs. Coleman and has already twined itself by its winning ways about their hearts.

Swan Motors is the new agency for Dodge cars and will soon announce an open house to display the new line at their South Miami Street garage.

J. B. King was appointed Station Master for the Wabash Railroad Express Depot. Mr. King has several years' experience in those duties at the Illinois Terminal.

Harold Price has announced he has opened a tailor shop at 224 South Wabash Street and is prepared to offer quality tailoring and umbrella repair to the public.

The G. M. Diehl Machine Works announces the addition of a foundry to its south Wabash factory.

Chapter 1

July 1935
Elks Lodge, Wabash, Indiana

THE THREE MEN WATCHED the condensation form on the outside of the tall glasses of draft beer, little driblets running down to form a pool of water at the base of the glasses on the table. The golden beer sparkled inside, so tempting on a hot day. Of the three, John Russell was the only one who truly appreciated the effect of the cold draft beer, for it was he who had insisted the Elks purchase the first refrigerated cooler in Wabash. It was much better than ice on this hot day in July. John had been the Exalted Ruler of the Elks last year, and it was a big honor to be the leader of the most important club in town. He wanted to make a change that all members would appreciate. It had been a big decision for the club to make in these depression times, and the new electric cooler was the result.

The other two men were club officers and had been a part of the process to purchase the cooler and have the old ice box torn out, even with some reluctance, after cooling beer with ice for over forty years. Garl Coleman, the present Exalted Ruler, was pleased with the results. The beer was colder, tasted fresher and was worth the tencent price. Frank Plum was the present Leading Knight and would be Exalted Ruler next year. By then, they would know how much the cooler cost to operate and if they would need to raise prices to cover the electric bill. The depression had hurt the membership; some had dropped out, and others were not having lunch as often. The five One Arm Bandit slot machines in the corner brought in enough cash to pay the help even with the gift to the local sheriff to look the other way.

The draft beer cost ten cents, and a large ham or roast beef sandwich with large pickle cost fifteen cents. A good light lunch could still be had for a quarter, leaving the afternoon to play cards with fellow members. It was a good place to spend time with your friends. You knew the men there would be the cream of the Wabash business and political life. Only the leaders were invited to become members of the Wabash Elks Lodge. That's the way it had always been, and that's the way it would stay.

That is—until this major problem came up. The meeting today among the three leaders of the club was the result of shocking bad news. The club received an application for membership from a person outside the circle of Wabash friends. This was not just any person, which would be easy to reject, just blackball the ballot box. No, this application was from that damned "shanty Irish" Democrat judge the governor appointed to fill the empty chair when Judge Murphy died unexpectedly.

Judge Murphy was "our" kind of Irish, "lace curtain Irish," whose Republican family had been a cornerstone in Wabash for a hundred years. He had been an active member of the Wabash Elks Club for many years. This new Judge McCowen was not "our" type of Irish citizen. Not at all. He was straight from Erie Point, the home of all the shanty Irish trash that vote straight Democrat in every election. The town of Erie Point was only seven miles east, but it was totally different from Wabash.

The town had been settled a hundred years before by Irish laborers who built the Erie Canal. They were mostly hard working, hard drinking and Irish Catholic—now Democratic citizens. A proud bunch, they built a flourishing town based on the rich surrounding farm community. But by the Depression in the 1930s, the town was just a shell of its former glory. The travelers on US 24 passed by the two-pump gas station, the dingy grill with the faded "EATS" sign, and the junk-filled garage that did car repair and fixed flat tires. They didn't see the neat, small town a block away, nestled along the Wabash River or the large Catholic church in the center of town, populated by a village of Irish citizens that were proud of their heritage: Irish, Catholic, and solid Democrat.

There had never been an application for membership from anyone in Erie Point before; it would have been quickly voted down and rejected. But this was different. This was the Wabash County Circuit Judge, a powerful man in local politics. It would be a bad move to reject the judge's application. That was a big problem.

The three men at the table were the cream of the crop, local Republican leaders in a strong Republican town. John Russell was the major stockholder and editor of the local newspaper, an important man in local business and politics. He lived the life of a small-town editor, playing his part and using his influence to the limit. His

The Gun from Dooley's Desk

appearance was that of a top businessman: a dark suit from Dick's Men's Wear, a fresh white shirt, a silk tie, and during the heat of the summer, a light Panama hat from Butch Howard's Men's Store. During the ten years he had owned the paper, he brought many changes to improve and expand the business.

Garl Coleman and his mother owned the major woodworking business in town, the Coleman Cabinet & Fine Furniture Factory. The Coleman family had started a mill shop in the 1850s, bringing in a water-powered sawmill and other woodworking machinery on the Erie Canal. After the Civil War, the company started making fine furniture for the expanding markets in the Midwest. During the 20s, with the advent of indoor plumbing and in-house kitchens, it started manufacturing kitchen cabinets.

Frank Plum, a lawyer and the local prosecuting attorney, was from one of the oldest pioneer families in Wabash County. His family had settled the north side of the river in the 1830s and had owned and controlled much of the development in the Wabash valley. His father and grandfather had been circuit court judges, and Frank had expected to be appointed judge, but the governor appointed that damn "Mick" instead.

In the following election, Judge McCowen beat Frank in a close contest. Now Frank would have to wait until the next election. Then he would win! He would finally claim and own what was rightfully his. Frank's rumpled appearance might have caused one to think he was a less able attorney, but many lawyers learned to their embarrassment in court that he was a top-notch lawyer, one of the best in the three-county area.

The three Elks officers had a lively discussion over lunch about this problem but did not come to any agreement, although each had definite ideas about what to do. Garl Coleman was worried about having the lodge vote on the judge.

"I'm afraid of all the bad publicity if a judge were blackballed and voted down. Half the county thinks he's great. We would look like a bunch of snobs, which we are not! Our rules are very selective; we just don't want some damn Mick from Erie Point. I don't even know him—I just know I don't want him in our club," he declared firmly.

Frank Plum lit his last Camel cigarette, crumpled the empty pack and remarked, "We are not going to lower our membership requirements. Our standards are high, only the best, and a "nobody Irish Mick" from Erie Point doesn't meet my standards. I don't care if he was appointed by that stupid-ass governor to be a temporary judge. He won the election and the longer he is in office, the better known he will become and the harder it will be to defeat him next time. He is a smooth talker, and he is building support with voters other than those in Erie Point. I don't want him in my club making new friends—next thing, he will want to bring in some other Erie Point trash with him. My answer is and will always be hell no—never—positively no!"

John Russell expressed his view. "You are right! I don't want any damn Mick in my lodge, especially that son of a bitch. He is getting to be the best-known Democratic politician in the county. We must do something damn soon. The judge has a brother in Erie Point who publishes a weekly paper named The Erie Point Free Press. I call it the yellow rag. I can imagine what that paper would write about the Elks if we blackballed that damn judge. It would make him the most popular man in the county. No, we cannot do that; we must find a way to make him withdraw the application for membership."

He looked around the taproom, a gentleman only area, with pride. At the back of the bar was a large mirror, tastefully painted with scenes along the beautiful Wabash River. There were sturdy wooden tables with captain's chairs, twenty comfortable leather stools at the bar, a larger table for groups and a heavy wooden pool table. To the side was the lounge with a large stone fireplace, a cheery place in the winter. There were several large leather lounge chairs for the members to relax, enjoy a drink and read the papers. The walls were paneled in burnished golden oak. Two lazy ceiling fans cooled the members during the summer.

John thought about the elegant dining room: crisp white tablecloths, the large white brick fireplace, and black metal wall lights bringing just the right amount of illumination to the room. There was no question the Elks Lodge was the top club in town. The members enjoyed real luxury in the depths of the depression. The thought of that shanty Irish judge entertaining his friends in "our" lodge irked John immensely.

"I'm going to check around to see if anything in the judge's background could be used to force him to withdraw. Everyone has something hidden in their past that they would like to keep secret, maybe the judge does also. I will try to dig up something we can use against him." John went on to say he would have a staffer at the paper go through the dead files to see if anything showed up from years past before he became judge. This would take a few days or more, but because it was July, the next Lodge meeting was not till September when the petition would be read on the Lodge floor.

Stewart approached the table with another round of beer. "Good afternoon, gentlemen. Is there anything else I can get you?" Distinguished and discreet, Stewart always wore a crisp white shirt with a bow tie, and he oversaw the running of the lodge with impeccable taste. He had been a fixture at the Elks for as long as anyone could remember.

Coleman glanced at the other two, and they shook their heads. "Thank you, Stewart. That will be all for today," Coleman said.

Frank had some news. "A new lawyer has opened an office in Erie Point, a young man named Bernie Flynn, whose parents own and operate the Erie Limestone Quarry in Erie Point. They supply lime rock to the new Rock Wool Insulation plant in Erie Point. It's the only business growing in the county. What the hell is rock wool? I hear you put it in your attic to keep the house warm in the winter. What will they invent next?" He picked up the crumpled Camel pack and tossed it in the wastebasket.

"I am glad I am not a new attorney just starting out during the Depression. It's tough as hell collecting cash now even from long time clients that we have known for

The Gun from Dooley's Desk

many years. This Depression is getting bad; some farmers are going to lose their land. It's tough and not going to get better anytime soon," Frank added.

The three men finished their lunch and after some idle passing of the local news, Frank told the latest joke about that son of a bitch, Franklin Roosevelt.

"He brought back beer, and what do you think? He taxed it so high, they couldn't drink."

They all smiled, but the new federal tax on beer was no joke. Frank got up to stretch his legs and stopped at the cigarette machine in the corner, put in a dime and got a new pack. He said to Garl, "The price of cigarettes is going up to two packs for a quarter; we may need to raise the price in the club's machine."

Garl replied, "That damn bunch in Washington put a new tax on cigarettes; before long a man can't afford to smoke. How can they do that?"

Russell drove back to the office, Coleman walked up the hill to his home on West Hill Street, while Frank stayed to play cards and have another beer or two at the club.

Chapter 2

WHILE THE THREE MEN at the Elks Club were discussing the man in the judge's office, the judge himself was in his courthouse office and had a different chain of thought. Judge M. Terrance McCowen was pleased with his progress to the circuit court. As he looked out the window overlooking the entire Wabash valley, he reflected on the past.

His was a humble beginning. Born and raised in Erie Point in a large Irish Catholic family, as a child he was quick and bright, and his mother taught him to read before starting school. His school was a one-room building housing all eight grades with one teacher where he excelled in all subjects. He was sent to a joint township high school because Erie Point did not have one. After high school, he attended and graduated from Huntington Day College. Later, he got a job in Huntington working in a local law firm as a clerk, "reading the law" as it was known.

After several years as a law clerk, he took the bar exam and passed the first try, a rare feat for a law clerk. He was certified as an attorney, practiced law with the Huntington firm to gain some experience and then opened a practice in Erie Point as the town's only attorney. McCowen ran on the Democratic ticket for the local township trustee position, was elected and served a term. He then ran in the county election for a seat on the Wabash County Council, and with solid local support of Erie Point Democrats, he was elected—the first Democrat to serve on the council in over thirty years. He gained a reputation as an honest, sharp attorney and as a shrewd politician. His power base was the solid backing from east Wabash County Democratic voters in Erie Point. He was their man and they loved him.

It came as a big surprise to him and the entire county when Judge Murphy died unexpectedly, and the Governor of Indiana appointed Terrance McCowen to serve as judge until the next election. He served with distinction and with his solid support was elected to a full term as Wabash Circuit Court Judge. He was a big man with an imposing look but a friendly handshake and a big Irish smile. He always dressed the part of a judge: black suit and vest, starched white shirt, a black string tie and on the bench, he wore the black robe. He was a strict, no-nonsense judge with a passion for the law.

Yet, after the session, he would have the attorneys in the case along with the court clerk Bob Miller back in his office for a little nip of Irish Dew and the latest joke or two. He earned the respect of the people who appeared in his court and other officers of the courthouse. McCowen and his wife were getting acquainted with Wabash society and meeting the most important as well as the less important members of the community.

Judge McCowen's wife Linda was about ten years younger and also a native of Erie Point. Her childhood was a troubled one as her father was Mike O'Dell, one of the local drunks who did odd jobs about town. Mike could not earn enough money to support his family and stay drunk, so he usually stayed drunk. His first real paid job came when he became the caretaker at the volunteer fire station. He was a practical man as far as politics went. He traded his vote on Election Day for ten wooden bar chips—good for ten tall draft beers at Dooley's Dive.

Their home was a small ramshackle house, a two bedroom with the outhouse out back—an inheritance from Mike's in-laws many years ago. The house was in a serious state of neglect, held together by the coat of light green paint applied many years ago. A Kelly green front door distinguished "the O'Dell place." The screen was gone from the back door for many years; Mike always said he would fix it "sometime soon." The enclosed back porch held a well-used Maytag wringer washer machine, two rinse tubs, and a stove to heat the water. Numerous wire clotheslines spanned the backyard for hanging the take-in washing.

His wife Jennie Hall O'Dell had worked hard her entire life to support her family of two girls, by working in a family's home when the wife went to have a baby and taking in washing and ironing for local families. Her desire was for her two girls to get out of Erie Point and have a better life than hers had been.

Linda's Aunt Phyllis, Mike O'Dell's sister, had gone to Huntington for high school and received her nurse's training at St. Joseph Hospital in Fort Wayne, graduating as an RN. She worked for a young doctor just starting a practice. Later she married Dr. Nagle, became his office

The Gun from Dooley's Desk

nurse, and together they built one of the largest medical practices in Huntington.

Linda had worked in Wabash for a wealthy family as a hired girl and later went to Huntington to live with her Aunt Phyllis. When she returned to Erie Point as a young lady, she started dating Terrance McCowen while he was a law clerk and reading the law. Later, when the law clerk became an attorney and had a few cases, they became engaged. Their wedding was in the century-old Catholic church, and everyone in Erie Point attended the real Irish wedding.

Times were tough for the new attorney and his young wife starting and building a law practice, but in time he succeeded. When Terrance was appointed circuit court judge, their life took a turn for the better. Linda volunteered at the church three days each week assisting the new priest Father Gibbons, and she played the organ for Mass. After being married for several years, she and the judge were still childless. Evidently, an operation for appendicitis in her teen years had rendered her unable to have children, the only flaw in the otherwise perfect Catholic family.

Linda's sister Lydia had also worked in Wabash for the same family with Linda, but she returned to Erie Point and later married John McCaffery from a large Catholic family. John was a few years older. He had married Rose Pickens, from a prosperous Catholic family—large farmers in east Wabash County. Together they had one child, John Michael McCaffery, who was still an infant when Rose was stricken with a rare type of blood infection causing her untimely death. John needed a mother for his son and a partner in life. Lydia was that perfect partner. She proved to be a loving mother, an affectionate wife, and a skillful business partner. Together they made a model Catholic family, and their business became a strong influence in the Erie Point community.

John's father operated the local funeral parlor McCaffery Mortuary Service in a small storefront, downtown near the church. John worked hard, graduated from Morticians Academy in Indianapolis and took over the family business. He purchased the largest home on Main Street in Erie Point and cleaned, painted and polished it until it sparkled. Soon, the McCaffery Funeral Home was conducting all the Irish funerals, carrying them to the Catholic cemetery north of town in the new black Packard Hearse.

His wife Lydia worked beside him in the business while they were raising their son John Michael McCaffery, whom everybody called Michael. They lived in the rear part of the large home, and the funeral parlor was in the front. Someone was on duty always. Lydia assisted John with the services, greeted the mourning families, played the pump organ and helped collect the accounts.

During the Depression, few families had life insurance, and most funeral bills were paid off a few dollars at a time. Often, a family would still be paying for the grandfather's funeral when the grandmother died. Then they made payments on both. Lydia was the bookkeeper for the funeral home, and as time went on, she frequently collected the rent money in person for the rental properties they owned. They also made farm

The Gun from Dooley's Desk

mortgages for the local farmers who could not get a loan at the Wabash banks.

She was an attractive lady, talented and strong-willed, and together with John, they made an attractive couple. When it came time for Terrance McCowen to campaign for elected office, all the members of the McCowen, McCaffery, O'Dell, and Pickens families in the eastern half of the county worked hard for his election. Many local families still owed money—most owed favors to them—all turned out and voted.

Terrance had an older brother Thomas McCowen, owner and editor of The Erie Point Free Press, a weekly Democratic newspaper and local printing shop. Thomas had a brilliant mind and a weakness for Irish whiskey, especially when someone else was buying. He also had a great talent in the printing trade, and some of his larger accounts were the Cole Brothers Circus in Peru and the Clyde Beatty Circus in Rochester.

Many of the brightly colored posters nailed on the light poles, depicting the snarling lions and the trumpeting elephants ridden by beautiful ladies in brief tights were printed in the Erie Point Print Shop by Thomas and his helper. There had been several times when the weekly paper came out a day late because the editor was sleeping off a hangover on the cot in the back room of the print shop. Most folks in Erie Point understood those little things happen and did not get too excited when the paper arrived the next day.

When Terrance campaigned for judge, a steady stream of printed material touting the Erie Point lawyer was produced, and the week before the election, a blanket mailing carrying a three-cent stamp was sent to every household in the entire county—a first in Wabash County politics. Many believed that this was the deciding factor in the election because there had not been a Democratic circuit judge in Wabash County in thirty-six years. The judge had a strong position, a strong family, and a strong community behind him.

He looked around his office with pride, taking in the details. His desk had a large desk folder, a large inkwell with a brass hinged cover, a glass paperweight and a small brass statue of the famous horse Dan Patch, the fastest racing horse in the world. As a young boy, he was impressed by a favorite uncle who came to visit. Uncle Joe helped train that famous harness racer in Oxford, Indiana. The world record set in 1909, a mile in 1.55, had not been broken yet in 1936. That horse was Indiana's most famous athlete.

On either side of the entrance door was a flag, the U.S. flag on the left and the flag of Indiana on the right. On the wall were the framed Bill of Rights and much to the embarrassment of the other courthouse officers, a picture of the president, Franklin Delano Roosevelt. The large oak wall clock announced the hours and half hours with a strong strike of the chimes. In the summer, when the windows were open, the only noise in the room would be the tick of the clock and the street noises filtering up from outdoors.

The sturdy oak bookshelves contained rows and rows of law books and official records needed to supply the court with legal information. The clerk accessed the highest shelves on a rolling ladder. The law filing system was installed in a rolling stand and was considered the standard of the time. A small alcove hid the hot plate, the coffee pot, and the judge's famous Jamaican roasted coffee stored in a metal canister.

He felt comfortable in his third-floor office in the courthouse, overlooking the police department's office and jail, the downtown city, and the entire river valley. Today, he was at the top of it all—the judge—the most respected position in the Wabash Courthouse. He felt rewarded; the struggle to get there was over.

Chapter 3

THE NEXT DAY, the new black Buick driven by John Russell pulled up in front of the office of the Erie Point Free Press and Printing Co., Thomas McCowen, Editor & Proprietor. The office was located next to the old canal locks at the edge of the town. John greeted Thomas warmly as men who respect each other's abilities. After a short visit, John and Thomas walked down to Dooley's for a bite of lunch. John bought lunch and several shots of whiskey that Thomas favored.

As they strolled back to the print shop/newspaper office, John stopped at his car and brought out a paper sack with a bottle of Jameson Irish Whiskey. Thomas produced two almost clean glasses, and the two of them spent the afternoon sipping whiskey, telling stories with John asking and learning about the old times in the town. Soon Tom was "drunk as a skunk" and later retired to the horsehair cot in the back room to sleep it off, a regular event at the print shop.

As John Russell drove back to Wabash along the new US 24 cement highway, he reflected on the day's events. He was proud of himself and his lunch with Tom McCowen at Dooley's Bar along with several shots of whiskey. Back at the shop that afternoon, they recalled

The Gun from Dooley's Desk

stories about events of local history and killed the bottle of Jameson's.

Tom loosened up and remembered stories of many years ago when he and Mike O'Dell would spend afternoons drinking together. "Mike told me one time about his girls and their experiences with a Wabash big shot who knocked up the older of the two. Mike boasted that he made the bastard pay. The pregnant teen went to Huntington to live with Mike's sister to have the kid; he didn't know what happened to it. Mike bragged his daughter is now married to a judge, and she has kept her family background a secret, but he knew. 'Damn, that was a long time ago; I should have got more money from that Wabash bastard, I bet he would have paid more.' Mike's boozed brain had speculated how much more cash this big shot bastard would pay for screwing his teenage girl and getting her pregnant. Too late now," Tom reflected. "It was a long time ago."

Tom's memory had faded as he fell into a deep drunken sleep. Russell led him to the back room, helped him onto the couch then walked out the front door, pulling down the "CLOSED" blind on the door and left. *What a day! This requires a visit to the Huntington Courthouse soon,* he thought. John went over what he had just learned from Tom. The oldest O'Dell girl is now Linda McCowen, wife of the judge. The McCowens don't have any children now, so the kid must have been given out to some family. That was not uncommon, it happened often, but where to start looking? The Huntington paper and birth records for sure.

What big news! He could hardly wait to tell Frank and Garl he had the goods that would make the judge withdraw the Elks application and not run for office again. He was very proud of his skills in working over that drunken bum Tom McCowen. He still had his reporter's touch; he could still dig up the facts. His new 1935 Buick purred along, gliding quietly over the new highway; the straight eight-cylinder engine was smooth and silent. *What an automobile!* The Buick Lady leading the way on the front hood and the Firestone white walls made it a top of the class automobile. John Russell had it all; he was at the top of his world.

The following day, Russell drove to Huntington to the office of the Huntington Daily News. He spent some time with his old friend Dan, the editor, and visited with the reporter who had covered the court news and local events for twenty-five years. That afternoon, he made a stop at the Huntington County Court to check some old birth records dating back to 1911, so old that they were kept in the archives storeroom. The clerk went back with him to the musty room where the old record books were kept.

He didn't know it, but the girl working at the clerk's office at the Huntington Courthouse, where he had checked birth records, was Patty Nagle, daughter of Phyllis O'Dell Nagle and the cousin of Linda O'Dell McCowen. The one name John Russell looked up at the clerk's office was Linda O'Dell. As soon as he left, Patty called her mother and reported the editor of the Wabash newspaper was making inquiries concerning a birth certificate in 1911 about a person named Linda O'Dell and signed by Dr. Nagle and Phyllis Nagle. Phyllis waited until after six o'clock to call Linda at Erie Point because it was cheaper to call long distance at night.

In the morning, both sisters, Linda McCowen and Lydia McCaffery, were on the morning Interurban streetcar from Erie Point to Huntington. Their Aunt Phyllis met them, and they went directly to the office of Dr. Nagle. Behind shut doors, they discussed the problem, and then Dr. Nagle went to the clerk's office and had his daughter show him the records that John Russell had requested.

Apparently, Russell had very good information about where to look in the old records because there it was: June 10, 1911, Birth baby girl, Mother Linda O'Dell, Age 16, Address unknown, Father unknown. The baby was named Lucille, no last name. The birth certificate was signed by Dr. Nagle, the delivering doctor and Phyllis Nagle, RN, the delivery nurse. A hand-written note on the bottom signed by the doctor suggested the baby was placed for adoption by private means. The doctor, in this case, was a very young Dr. Nagle in his second year of practice.

Dr. Nagle recalled the night as if it were yesterday. They left the hospital by the back door. The young mother was huddled in the back seat with his wife, holding the baby in her arms. They drove to the Nagle home, put the young mother to bed in the guest bedroom, and when she was asleep, he and Phyllis drove to Wabash to deliver the baby to its new parents. The doctor was very concerned; the Indiana law about baby selling and private placement of children was very strict.

Several years earlier, a group of doctors had been exposed selling babies. Soon the case swelled into a major headline-grabbing scandal. Nine doctors lost their medical licenses and two went to prison. New strict state laws were passed. All placements now had to be approved by the circuit judge and recorded. Doctor and Phyllis had discussed this in hushed tones. They agreed this was different, the baby's mother was Doctor and Phyllis' niece, but still, it was not a legal adoption.

Only the doctor and Phyllis knew where the baby went—they never told anyone. *No one will ever know.*

The family that received the baby believed they were blessed by a gift from heaven. It had been over twenty-three years since this happened, but now the cat was out of the bag.

. . .

It was a common practice for young girls from Erie Point to be placed in homes of well to do families in Wabash. They helped with the cooking, cleaning, and washing. They were referred to as hired girls. Sometimes they helped the lady of the house, and sometimes they helped the maid. Often, the same girl would stay there for several years as a live-in while the family maid would be a day person. Now that the depression was in full bloom, very few families could keep a full-time day maid, but many families kept a live-in hired girl.

The two O'Dell sisters had been live-in hired girls in their teenage years. Their family always needed the money as their father drank up all his pay at the taverns in Erie

Point. They survived on the income from the sisters and the cash his wife Jennie made from taking in washing and ironing for people. The girls worked for a wealthy family on West Hill Street in Wabash usually staying a full month before going home. The sisters were homesick to see their mom.

The family they worked for was the Coleman family: Garl Coleman Sr. and his wife Grace, Garl Coleman II and his wife Sarah. Garl was an only child, and Sarah did not bring forth any heir in their several years of marriage. When Garland Sr. died in the summer of 1909, Garl Coleman II, then 25 years old, took over the furniture manufacturing business and the house. His wife and his mother simply obeyed his every wish and command.

Garl employed a maid two days a week and kept the O'Dell girls full time. By 1911, he had achieved much. He had expanded the factory building, added new machinery and equipment, designed a new furniture and cabinet line, printed a new catalog, remodeled the kitchen at the house, purchased the town's newest Oldsmobile automobile and had 16-year-old Linda O'Dell pregnant.

His solution to that problem was to drive Linda back to the O'Dell house in Erie Point, present her to her father and tell him that she was slipping out at night to see a neighborhood good for nothing boy and had got herself pregnant. Before taking her home, he took Linda aside and warned her.

"If you tell anyone about what happens each Thursday afternoon in your bedroom, I will see to it that you and your sister will be sent to White's Institute until you are both twenty-one years old, and your family will not have the right to visit you!"

The two girls were young and uneducated. They had been warned by their father that they must do whatever the Colemans wanted them to do. They were both terrified when they discovered Mr. Coleman was spying on them from a hole in the back closet where he kept his overcoat, raincoat, and umbrella. They discovered the peephole one day when putting away the Hoover sweeper in the closet next to their room. Each Thursday afternoon, while Mrs. Coleman was at the Lady's Club playing bridge, Mr. Coleman would come home after lunch, call the girls into their room and order them to undress before him. When they were naked, he would admire and feel their firm little bodies and have sex with one and sometimes both terrified girls.

Linda, being older and more developed, seemed his favorite, and he abused her often. She cried because he hurt her but was too afraid and ashamed to tell anyone. After several weeks, the girls felt so threatened by him, they told their mother they did not want to go back to Wabash to stay at the Coleman house. They were afraid to tell her why, and they were in tears. Their dad ordered them to return and mind what the Colemans said. Their pay was given to him, and it added to the family income, but some he spent at Dooley's bar where he was a regular patron.

They returned to the Coleman home, and later that week Linda missed her period and started being sick every morning, throwing up, too weak to work. Mr. Coleman took her to the family doctor, who ran some tests and

The Gun from Dooley's Desk

informed Garl she was pregnant. Now it was Coleman who was terrified. But he was a man of action. He drove Linda back to the O'Dell house in Erie Point, and before they got out of the car, he warned her again. Coleman told her if she told anyone about this, he would see to it that Mike lost his job at the fire station. Garl Coleman was a powerful man in Wabash County, and she was positive he could and would do it. Coleman gave Mike and Jennie $50.00 cash and agreed that there would be another $50.00 if everything went right. They understood exactly, do what they were told.

Jennie called Phyllis and made arrangements for Linda to live in the Nagle home until the baby was born. When they were ready to leave for the Nagle home, the O'Dell's car would not start; the battery was dead. Coleman reluctantly agreed to drive Linda to Huntington. There he met Phyllis and Dr. Nagle who understood exactly what had happened to Linda. No words were spoken, but Linda conveyed the message that it was Coleman who was the perpetrator of this sorry mess. She was terrified of him and displayed her fear of the powerful man.

Dr. Nagle and Phyllis were outraged at Coleman's conduct: bringing this young girl whom he impregnated, paying her father hush money and dropping her off with relatives like a dog at the city pound for someone else to keep and bring forth the unwanted child. Phyllis called Jenny and had a serious discussion with her resulting in Lydia being permanently removed from the Coleman home.

While driving back to Wabash, Garl was relieved all this unpleasantness was over. His life could now get back to normal. *Forget that damn girl—the little bitch!* He was glad she was gone. *No one will ever know.*

The Nagles were uncomfortable. They felt that Coleman needed to receive his due judgment—but how? He was a powerful man, had a lot of influence and had friends in powerful places. They knew something had to be done—but what? Phyllis and her husband had several long discussions about what to do now. Phyllis knew a little about the Coleman household from talking to the girls when visiting her sister's home on the weekends. She was determined to make Garl Coleman pay to raise this child and see the results of his depravity every day. Together they devised a plan and agreed to carry it out. After the child was born, they would deliver it to the Coleman home and leave it in a basket on the front step. The only information would be the baby's name. This was a dangerous and illegal action, but they carried it out together. *No one will ever know.*

Linda stayed with her aunt, attended school and in time delivered a healthy baby girl whom she named Lucille after a very popular song of the time. Three days later, after leaving the hospital, the baby was taken for adoption. Linda never heard of the little girl again. Linda lived with the Nagle family, attended Huntington High School and after graduation, moved back home to Erie Point.

. . .

The Gun from Dooley's Desk

The Coleman family underwent a sudden and spectacular change that warm June morning due to an event that shocked the family and was the talk of the town. The newspaper carried a story about the unusual event, a baby on the doorstep. Sarah Coleman could not have children, and this was a very sad part of her life. She was the only child of Frank and Helen King and had inherited the entire King estate. This included two large farms and several grain elevators along the old Erie Canal, now along the railroad, plus a large Wabash coal yard. Not having an heir was a great concern to her. She had talked to their minister about adopting a baby, but nothing suitable had been found.

Her prayers were answered that morning when she opened the front door of the West Hill Street home to get the milk delivery and found a baby in a basket at the door. The note said her name was Lucille. The mother could not keep her and wished the baby to have a good Christian home. Sarah understood this was an act of God, an answer to their prayers, delivering this beautiful baby girl to their home. She opened her heart, and soon Lucille was the center of attraction in the Coleman home.

The family doctor examined the child and declared her hale and hearty. The room next to the master bedroom was turned into a nursery. In no time at all, Baby Lucille was the center of the world for the Coleman family. The Colemans had inquiries made in the Wabash area to see if the parents of this baby could be located but with no results.

Before the baby was two years old, Sarah insisted they legally adopt the child. The Law Office of Plum & Plum took care of the details, and the court approved the adoption. The baby was now legally Lucille King Coleman and someday would be the heir to both the King and the Coleman fortunes. But for now, she was just Little Lucy Coleman, the sweetheart who captured the hearts of all on West Hill Street.

The Gun from Dooley's Desk

Chapter 4

NOW, TWENTY-FOUR YEARS LATER, John Russell learned about the judge's wife having an illegitimate baby when she was a teenager and that Dr. Nagle had arranged an illegal adoption with no records where the baby was placed. This was important information, but it had to be used very carefully. It was not uncommon for an unmarried young girl to go to her out of town relatives to have a baby, but usually there was some trail of where the baby was adopted. Newspapermen had a way of digging through hospital and court records, even those sealed by a judge, and finding the facts. In this case, the baby disappeared, and no records were found of the final adoption. This could get Dr. Nagle in serious legal trouble even though it had happened over twenty years ago.

Dr. Nagle was a respected physician, and no court would convict him of child stealing and selling the baby as some doctors had done in years past, but it would ruin his reputation as the local family doctor in the Huntington community. Because the doctor and his wife were the child's uncle and aunt, it was possible the child was raised in one of the large Irish families in Erie Point. Russell figured another Irish bastard would not be noticed in a town that had several kids who were not certain of their real parents.

The Gun from Dooley's Desk

No, this could not be a legal case. It needed to be handled as a way to threaten the judge with exposure of his wife's background, one thing that would ruin her reputation and embarrass the proud family. This could be used to force the judge to withdraw the Elks application and to threaten to use it against him if he were to run for judge again. *If we could find that kid, it would be really bad news for the judge,* Russell mused. *Surprise Judge! Meet your wife's daughter.*

The next morning, he called Frank Plum and Garl Coleman to meet him at the Elks for lunch as he had some exciting information to share with them.

"Sorry, my wife and I are just leaving for the cottage at Silver Lake. We will be gone a week, so I can't make it for lunch. We will meet next Monday to get your news," Frank replied.

John Russell and Garl Coleman met at their usual table in the corner of the taproom. John related the information he had developed about the judge's wife having an illegitimate child in Huntington and the child disappearing after birth. John was excited he learned this important news, but Garl was suddenly distracted. The name O'Dell rang a bell in his mind. O'Dell was the name of the girls working at his home many years ago. He remembered taking the pregnant girl to Erie Point and paying off that drunken bum father with cash. He had never heard anything about the baby.

Garl tried to remember the details of the two girls. He remembered when he took the eldest home but could not remember their first names. His mind was reeling when he realized this baby could be the child he fathered with that hired girl many years ago. *My God! I will be branded a child molester, preying on helpless young girls—the worst kind of predator. How could this happen to a Christian man like me? Their little, naked bodies enticed me to do what I did. What bad luck. Damn her—it's her fault, damn little bitch!*

All of this came like a bolt out of the blue. It made Garl sick to his stomach; his life would be ruined—the family devastated. Some way, he had to stop John from releasing this information in this campaign to embarrass the judge. Keeping him out of the Elks was not worth ruining his life and the Coleman family's reputation. The embarrassment of it all would turn his daughter away from him. Something had to be done! Russell wanted to meet with the judge the next day and confront him with the news, but Garl quickly put a stop to it.

"No. We agreed to work together. Let's wait until Frank gets back next week. Then the three of us will meet and confront the judge with this bad news."

John reluctantly agreed, much to Garl's relief. That night, Garl stayed up late worrying about what to do. The situation was hopeless, and he had only a week to find a solution. A desperate man will do desperate things.

· · ·

That same night, the lights burned late at the rear office of Dr. Nagle. He and Phyllis knew the information John Russell gleaned from the court and hospital records was not complete and he would be back asking questions. Russell would want to know where the child was taken for adoption. They did not know what he wanted to do with

The Gun from Dooley's Desk

this information, but it certainly would not be good for the doctor. It could be used by the state medical board to strip him of his medical license, and if not that, could be turned over to the prosecuting attorney for legal action. It had been a dumb thing to do, but at the time they were inexperienced and did their best in a bad family situation.

Now it was coming back to haunt them, perhaps ruin them. The least that could happen would be the loss of his license and his practice, the most prominent physician in Huntington ruined. The worst would be arrest, a trial, and perhaps jail. Dr. Nagle and Phyllis were desperate to find a solution. Phyllis felt responsible for this problem, and a desperate woman will take desperate actions.

On the Interurban streetcar back to Erie Point, Linda McCowen and her sister Lydia McCaffery carried on a hushed conversation about the day's event. Both women were upset about this news and felt sick, remembering the Thursday afternoons with Garl Coleman. Linda guessed the newspaper editor was after information that would hurt the judge and embarrass him in an election. She did not know where the baby was taken and was amazed anyone would be interested after twenty-four years. It seemed unusual the editor himself would come to Huntington to seek the information.

It was a strange coincidence that Phyllis' daughter was working in the clerk's office when John Russell came in to check the records. Linda had never told her husband about her teenage pregnancy and the baby's birth. He had been in college while she was in high school, and he thought she went to Huntington to go to school as there was no high school in Erie Point. Linda did not want her husband to find this out, especially by some newspaperman who wanted to destroy the judge and embarrass the family. When they arrived in Erie Point, Linda stopped at the church, burned a candle and prayed at the darkened altar. She was desperate to find a solution that would keep her secret and protect the most cherished thing in her life, her husband. She prayed for help.

Lydia stopped by Dooley's to collect the rent, but Charley Dooley was on an errand when she arrived, so she waited in the back office until he returned. Ladies did not go to Dooley's Dive, so Lydia went in the back door and waited in the office for Mr. Dooley. When Charley arrived, he unlocked the safe and counted out the rent in cash as was the custom. She signed the receipt and put the cash in her large purse.

After having some small talk, she thanked Mr. Dooley and walked the four blocks to the funeral home where they lived. She greeted her husband and declared, "My sister and I had a great visit with Aunt Phyllis. We promised to get together more often to catch up on family activities. Dr. Nagle and Phyllis are about to buy a building for their new office near the hospital. It will be a great move for them. The price was right, a little more than what is owed in taxes."

The Gun from Dooley's Desk

Chapter 5

FRIDAY AFTERNOON WAS a typical summer day: pleasant, not too hot, just pleasing. John Russell left the newspaper office early in the afternoon, drove the new Buick home, carefully parked in the garage and walked toward his house. The garage was in the back of the lot on the alley next to the railroad tracks. The big house faced West Hill Street and was some distance from the back alley. The brick paved walk to the house was partially covered by a grape arbor, laden with ripe purple grapes, buzzing with bees.

Next to the back door was a brick patio containing a green garden bench with oak slats. The trellises behind the bench were overflowing with blooming morning glories cascading down to a sea of pink, red, and white petunias, completely covering the ground around the garden bench. It was a lovely little secluded spot to sit in the shade, enjoy the flowers and sip a cool refreshing drink.

John walked up the brick walk, happy to be home, thinking of a cool whiskey on the rocks he would soon enjoy at the garden bench. As he approached the back door, he realized two people were sitting on the bench. His first thought was that they were the yard people hired

The Gun from Dooley's Desk

to mow and rake the yard each week. Then he noticed a large shopping bag on the brick path near their feet.

He was ready to speak to them, but they both stood, and one lifted his right hand. John saw the silver revolver just as it fired directly in his face. His body recoiled back from the impact, twisted and brushed against the second person before falling on his back in the petunias. The single shot had dropped him dead on the spot with a massive head wound. Not a word had been spoken.

• • •

Jimmy Johnson was a twelve-year-old boy who attended Miami School in Wabash and delivered papers for the Wabash Daily News. Jimmy was a friendly kid who spent most of his time riding his bike about town. Summer or winter, he always wore his Lindberg helmet and goggles. His route included many of the local businesses: the hotel, Bill's barbershop, many of the courthouse offices as well as the local pool hall and Blackie's bookie joint.

Jimmy knew many people in town, and most residents recognized the boy in the helmet and goggles riding the red Schwinn bicycle. That special bike had a large wire basket on the handlebars, the horn headlight, the mud-flap with a red reflector and a squirrel's tail hanging from each handle grip. The bike was Jimmy's greatest possession, purchased new for $24.99 at Gamble's Hardware Store from the profits of his large paper route.

Jimmy was eager to get his paper route delivered quickly that day. At five o'clock, his favorite radio program would be on WOWO. "Jack Armstrong, the All-American Boy" was the top radio program for boys. Jimmy listened every week for the latest mystery, solved by the actions of his hero, Jack Armstrong. *If I were older, I would be like Jack Armstrong,* Jimmy thought as he tossed the paper onto Mrs. Cline's front porch, near the front door.

He was delivering on West Hill Street to the large houses that lined the street, fronted by tall elm trees that provided shade and shelter for the sidewalk. He went back and forth, to the Baker's, across to the Perkins', back across to the Coleman's, across to the Smith's, then skip two and deliver the Brown's then the Russell home. He was careful with that one and put it in the paper box. Russell was the owner of the paper; you had to get it right when dealing with the boss. Jimmy continued down the road to Thorne Street, turned north to the two houses there then turned east down the unpaved alley back to Ross Street. After Ross, he headed home—done—now it was radio time. That was the normal schedule, but today something was a little different, an incident that would have a big effect on Jimmy's life.

Jimmy had finished Thorne Street, turned east into the alley along the railroad and returned behind the West Hill Street homes. One of the residents had put out the junk to be picked up by the city truck. Things like this were of supreme interest to a kid, especially Jimmy. He parked his bike next to the shrubs behind the garage and examined the boxes of discarded stuff. While engaged in this important discovery process, he heard a sharp noise nearby. He listened but heard nothing more. He returned

The Gun from Dooley's Desk

to examining the boxes when he noticed two people walk rapidly down the alley and enter the Coleman garage. That seemed a little strange, but he had more important things to do. He selected several small items, put them in his paper bag, mounted his bike and continued down the alley.

Jimmy had not gone far when he heard the crunch of a car behind him, and he pulled over on the lawn to allow the car to pass. He recognized the blue Oldsmobile with Mr. Coleman driving, but the passenger in the front seat was not Mrs. Coleman. He did not know the woman although he saw her from a few feet as the car slowly passed him in the narrow part of the alley. He had delivered papers in that neighborhood a long time and knew all the women by sight including the maids that worked in some homes. This lady with auburn hair was no one he had seen before. Jimmy hurried to finish his route and get home in time for another exciting episode of "Jack Armstrong, the All-American Boy, brought to you by Wheaties, the All-American Breakfast Cereal."

• • •

Later that afternoon, Officer Parker, "Big Billy" as he was known, stared into the flowers under the morning glory vines at the body crumpled there. With him was Morris, the custodian from the Methodist church and one of the few black men in Wabash. Morris had been pushing his bicycle with a flat tire down West Hill Street when he heard a loud noise, like a shot. He stopped, looked into the Russell yard and saw two men in old clothes walking away with their backs to him. They appeared to be hobos. They walked toward the alley, and when they reached the alley, they turned east. One was carrying a large shopping bag.

Something did not look right to Morris, and he walked over to look. He had worked for the Russell family several times doing yard work and spring cleaning, and he was familiar with the back entrance of the house. He looked at the door and didn't see anything wrong. As he turned to go back to his bicycle, he saw the shoe soles and feet of a man lying on the ground in the flower bed in front of the morning glory vines. One look at the face and he knew the man had to be dead. He rushed to the side door, shouted and knocked hard, but he could see no one was home at the Russell's. He ran to the house next door where the retired dentist lived and pounded on the door.

"Help! Call the police station! There is a dead man in the flowers. Get someone quick. Oh, my God, this is terrible."

The call was received by one of the firemen who sometimes answered the phone. The fireman called Billy Parker's home because he was supposed to be the officer on duty. He was having a late lunch. Billy had the only police car and raced to the Russell home. There he met the nervous Morris and Dr. Davis from next door. Billy did not recognize the dead man, but because no one was home at the Russell house, he suspected it might be John Russell. He went next door to Dr. Davis' house and phoned Chief Zeno Moore at home. The chief called State Police Detective Deamer to meet him at the Russell home and then rushed to the West Hill Street house.

The Gun from Dooley's Desk

Their investigation determined that it was the body of John Russell and that he had been shot in the face at point-blank range, dying instantly. The body was removed to the Johnson Funeral Home three blocks away. Careful examination concluded his gold Hamilton watch was still in his vest pocket, and his wallet containing money was not taken. The diamond stickpin in his tie and the diamond ring on his finger were still intact. If robbery was the motive, nothing was stolen. The only thing amiss was a broken, short gold chain where men normally wore a watch fob.

Later that afternoon at the funeral home, Mrs. Russell tearfully identified the body, declared it to be that of her husband John Russell and confirmed all his possessions except one were present. The missing item was his favorite, his elk's tooth he wore on his watch chain; it had hung on the broken, short chain. The gold trimmed elk's tooth was a gift from his lodge brothers. Last year he had been Exalted Ruler of the local Elks Lodge. He was very proud of it and wore it on his watch chain dangling in front of his vest buttons. Apparently, that was the only item that could not be accounted for by the police. The police made a very thorough investigation of the neighborhood; none of the neighbors heard or saw anything unusual. Mrs. Russell and her mother had been volunteering at the hospital when the murder occurred; they could shed no light on anyone that may have had a reason to shoot John Russell.

On the second day of the investigation, the police arrived at the conclusion the murder was a botched burglary attempt. They believed the home was empty.

Two hobos came up the back alley, watched the house and seeing no activity, they decided to break in the back door. As they were attempting to force the door, John Russell walked up behind them. They panicked, and one burglar shot Russell in the face. The hobos then ran down the walkway to the alley and escaped toward the railroad track.

An investigation of the train schedule showed a slow-moving freight train, headed west to Peru, had come through town about this time. Obviously, the hobo burglars—now murderers—caught the train, and by the time the police arrived at the crime scene, they had been halfway to the Peru railroad yards. The police departments of the towns and cities in the area were contacted to be on the lookout for two men riding the rails.

The Peru Police Department sent both police cars with local policemen to the hobo camp at the end of the railroad switchyard to make a sweep of all the tramps and hobos camping there. The search turned up two men who fit the description of the wanted men. Both were well known to the police in Peru, Wabash, and Huntington as they rode the train to those towns begging, stealing or living in hobo camps along the way.

The older man Junior Bill Banks was a drinker who drank anything containing alcohol. He drank Muscatel wine when he had some money, Brilliantine hair dressing when he was broke or local home brew when he could work in exchange for booze. During the winter, Junior would often go to the local jail when he was drunk and had no place to sleep. The jailer would let him sleep it off for a couple of days before he threw him out again. They sometimes took him to the city limits and sent him on his way. Every policeman and jailer in all the towns along the Wabash Railroad knew Junior Billy Banks very well.

The other suspect was Jerry Lester, a local unemployed drifter, who came from a well-known circus family in Peru. Jerry Lester grew up in the circus world, spending most of his early years traveling with his folks, who were performers and animal trainers, on the circus train through the central and southern part of the country. When the Depression put most of the circuses out of business, several put down roots in the towns where they had wintered. The Wallace Circus stayed in the Peru area, and the Clyde Beatty Circus stayed in Rochester a few miles north.

There was no work for Jerry, so he bummed out and rode the rails here and there to find day to day work. Jerry was a petty thief and stole anything he could carry. He had never learned to drive and depended on the empty freight car as his transportation. He spent most of his money on cheap red wine and had been arrested several times for drunk and disorderly conduct including one time in Rich Valley for attempting to break into the office of the grain elevator. Jerry spent six months at the State Farm for that offense, which established his criminal record but never had been charged with any kind of violent crime.

The further investigation proved that Junior Billy Banks had an alibi; he had been in the Huntington jail the day of the murder. The other suspect Jerry Lester claimed he was innocent but had no alibi. He had been seen in the Wabash area with some other men on the day the crime was committed. Jerry was held at the Peru jail on a vagrancy charge pending further investigation. A meeting with the chief of police, the state police detective appointed to the case and the prosecuting attorney was held to determine the next action to take.

The murder weapon was a large caliber, like a .38, but no weapon had been found although a thorough search along the railroad tracks had been conducted. Several witnesses claimed to have seen Jerry Lester and some other men in the West Hill Street area that day. Jerry Lester had run away to Peru where he was apprehended, and he had a record. The chief believed Jerry Lester to be a strong suspect, and if he could talk to him, he might confess. Prosecuting Attorney Frank Plum petitioned the court to issue extradition papers to bring Lester to the Wabash Jail to be held and investigated in the murder of John Russell.

Judge Terrance McCowen issued the order, and Chief Moore and Billy Parker drove the new Plymouth police car to Peru to pick up the suspect, a fourteen-mile trip. The return trip to Wabash proved to be an exciting time for the police officers and made the chief a hero. While driving back, the suspect said he needed to relieve himself, so they pulled off the road in a remote spot of woods. They all got out of the car to take a leak.

The suspect attempted to escape, and in the process of recapturing him, the chief was required to use force, and the suspect was injured. Lester was taken to the Wabash County Hospital for examination before being booked into jail. At the jail, he was interrogated for several days by Chief Moore and Officer Billy Parker, still, Lester denied everything. After a late evening visit with the chief,

The Gun from Dooley's Desk

the suspect signed a two-page confession written for him by Chief Zeno Moore and witnessed by Officer Parker.

The next day, he was charged with murder based on his signed confession. The city was relieved now that the murderer was in jail. The newspaper praised the police work of the chief, his assistant, the state police officer, and prosecuting attorney for the prompt way the murder was solved. The only other murder in Wabash County was twenty years before, a drunken brawl where a local good for nothing shot another good for nothing over some good for nothing woman. This ruthless murder of one of the city's most important citizens was an event of major concern. Now it was over—the culprit was in custody, had confessed and awaited trial.

Chapter 6

TWO WEEKS LATER, Jimmy was in the same alley beside the railroad tracks, looking in some of the trash cans. Not finding anything of great interest, he rode on to the end of the alley behind the church. There, something on the ground in the thorn bushes caught his sharp eye. He parked his bike, carefully reached into the sharp thorn bushes and pulled out a real gun—a nickel-plated Iver Johnson .38 caliber revolver with black grips and fully loaded. Like any twelve-year-old boy, he was fascinated with guns, and he knew enough about them to know this gun was real, was loaded and was a very valuable possession. He hid the gun in a paper bag and hurried to finish his route. At supper, he was in such a hurry to finish, his mother was concerned.

Jimmy's dad said, "It's just a phase he's going through."

Up in his room, he examined his new find very carefully, removing the four loaded cartridges and the empty brass shell. He wiped it clean even polished off a little rust spot on the hammer. He said to himself, "It's a real gun, and it's all mine." Everyone knew the Law of Kids: Finders keepers (Losers weepers.) Like all boys, Jimmy could not keep a secret as big as this to himself, so he bragged to the neighbor girl to impress her. She said

The Gun from Dooley's Desk

she didn't believe him, so he showed her the gun. That evening, she told her dad, and he told Jimmy's dad. Jimmy's dad took the gun and was going to throw it in the trash but instead gave it to a neighbor down the street who was a city policeman.

The policeman gave it to Chief Moore and told him who found it. The chief called Jimmy's parents and told them he needed to know exactly where the gun was found. Jimmy hoped some of his friends would see him riding in the front seat of the police car. He wished the chief would run the siren! The chief drove to the alley behind the church where Jimmy pointed out the exact spot. Chief Moore was positive the murder weapon had been found, and the empty shell was from the bullet that killed John Russell.

The Wabash Daily News had a front-page story about finding the gun with a large picture of Jimmy on his bicycle pointing to the bushes behind the church and the chief holding the nickel-plated gun. A large close-up picture of the Iver Johnson Safety Hammer Double Action Revolver was displayed along with the story that the police did not know where Lester got the gun. Jimmy's mom bought ten copies of the paper to send to all the relatives to show them what a big hero young Jimmy was with his picture on the front page of the paper.

DOOLEY'S EMPORIUM
Dispenser of Fine Wine & Spirits

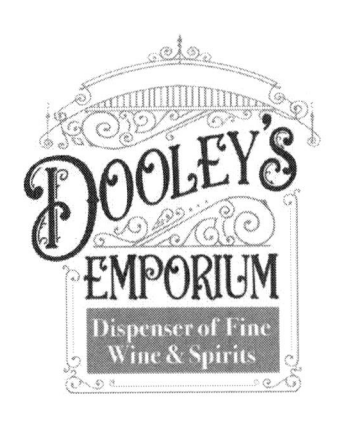

In Erie Point the next day, Charley Dooley was reading the paper while drinking his morning coffee. He carefully looked at the picture of the revolver before he went to the back office at Dooley's Bar to check the hiding place of his nickel-plated Iver Johnson .38 revolver. He opened the lower door of the oak roll top desk, pulled out the wooden box where the gun was hidden—the gun was gone!

Charley was the owner of Dooley's Emporium, Dispenser of Fine Wine and Spirits, known locally in Erie Point as "Dooley's Dive," a Saturday night cut and shoot place. The nondescript, red brick building with a gray slate roof was situated downtown on the corner of Main and Canal Street, a block from the railroad tracks. It was built in the late 1890s. A small sign on the door stated, "UNESCORTED WOMEN NOT ALLOWED." Charley firmly enforced that rule.

The inside was just as exciting as the exterior. Small wooden tables and well-abused chairs were placed in the main area. Next was a three-sided bar with eight fixed barstools. The back bar was a large mirror with a painting of a reclining voluptuous lady, welcoming all the rowdy male patrons of the bar who fantasized the exciting time such a lady would provide. Over the bar was a faded sign: "MAY YOUR TROUBLES BE LESS AND YOUR BLESSINGS REACH FAR, MAY THERE ALWAYS BE JAMESON'S STOCKED AT THE BAR."

Mrs. Fritchy ran the kitchen, serving lunch and dinner. Her specialty was real Irish stew, made like her mother taught her, the real way. Hers was the best Irish stew west of New York—she would tell you so herself.

The dishwasher was usually some hobo drifter passing through. After a few weeks, he would move on and catch the local freight train for the next town.

Charley was the best-known man in town. He ran a tough place, but when the fighting got too rough inside, Charley would grab his shillelagh, bang a few hard, Irish heads and throw the hooligans out in the street. Sometimes they kept on fighting and got the local street dogs involved, barking and snarling. The town marshal would knock some sense into their heads with a large walnut nightstick. When they sobered up, they were the best of friends until the next Saturday night when it happened all over again.

An honest man in a tough town, trouble with the law was the last thing Charley wanted or needed. He walked to the office of young Attorney Bernie Flynn and discussed what to do about reporting the ownership of the gun. Bernie determined that Charley would not be in trouble because the gun was stolen from him by persons unknown. Bernie Flynn picked up the telephone and called long distance to the Wabash Police Station.

Shortly, the new Wabash City Police car was speeding toward Erie Point with the siren screaming, Chief Moore at the wheel. Frank Plum held on for dear life as they sped around the curves and over the hills to Erie Point. The men entered the office of B. J. Flynn, Attorney at Law, and Bernie informed them that he represented Mr. Charles Dooley and would be present during any questioning.

Mr. Dooley explained that earlier in the previous summer, Jerry Lester had worked cleaning up the yard at the tavern and had slept in the shed behind the tavern for several nights. Charley had offered him work, food, and a place to sleep as he did other hobos and out of work drifters who happened by. Jerry Lester was no different than most; he stayed and worked several days then one morning caught the local freight-train and moved on.

Charley had not seen Jerry Lester since and did not know the gun was missing, nor did he know for certain that Lester took it. However, he knew Lester was a thief and would steal anything he could carry to sell in the next town in exchange for food and booze. The chief was positive now that they had connected the stolen gun to Jerry Lester, and Frank Plum knew that Mr. Dooley would make a strong witness. They were both feeling good about the coming trial as they drove back to Wabash.

. . .

The Gun from Dooley's Desk

The trial had been set for November 1935, but now the suspect was hospitalized with a ruptured spleen, and it was put off until the January 1936 session. The court appointed the newest member of the Wabash legal profession to represent the defendant, a young Joseph Sloop. The trial was held in the circuit courtroom, Judge Terrance McCowen presiding. The room was a symbol of authority: impressive, solid, mahogany desks and chairs, the judge's elevated desk and the rich wall paneling behind, the paneled jury box, the chairs with black leather upholstery and the witness box with the large Bible on the stand. The sharp contrast of the bright colors of the American flag against the dark mahogany paneling was striking. This was the ideal setting for the right of every American—a speedy and fair trial before a jury of your peers.

Prosecutor Frank Plum presented a solid case: many good strong witnesses, the gun, the train schedule, the fact the defendant had a police record and most importantly, the confession, signed by Jerry Lester. Chief Moore was a good witness. He swore the confession was given willingly, dictated to him by Jerry Lester. Officer Parker testified he had witnessed the confession and that Lester signed it.

Joseph Sloop had little to work with; the defendant was a bum with a police record, a known drunk and a proven liar. The recanted confession was in doubt because few believed their appointed chief of police would do the things that Lester accused him of. Chief Moore was a man of good repute, a local man who had been a football player and graduated from Wabash High School many years before. He attended the Falls Avenue Church, his kids attended local schools, and his wife worked for a local optometrist. Chief Moore was the salt of the earth.

The jury deliberated from ten o'clock until noon when the judge sent them under the protection of the court bailiff to the Rock City Restaurant for lunch. Later, the foreman said they had already reached the verdict but wanted to get a free lunch for their trouble serving on this jury. After returning to the courtroom, the foreman gave the bailiff the written verdict. The bailiff passed it to the court clerk who read it to the court. Guilty as charged—the death sentence recommended. The jury members were polled, and all agreed.

Judge McCowen ordered the defendant delivered to the State Prison at Michigan City and there be put to death in the electric chair. The defendant would be returned to the County Jail until such time as he could be transported to the Michigan City Prison. It was over, the city's most dastardly crime resolved. The scales of justice were back in balance again. The city returned to normal day to day functions—the crisis was over.

. . .

Several days later after a busy court day, the judge, the clerk, and the prosecutor were meeting informally in the judge's chambers. The judge had produced a bottle of good whiskey, and the three men were enjoying a little nip along with some good stories. The judge was an excellent storyteller and told a new joke that produced some hearty laughs. The group was enjoying the jovial mood when

The Gun from Dooley's Desk

they heard a loud commotion outside the judge's window on the street below. They went to the window to see Chief Moore rush out of the jail, run across the street and run up the two long flights of steps to the courthouse porch. They heard the door swing open with a bang and the chief running up the three flights of marble steps to the courtroom floor, shouting incoherently at the top of his voice.

They rushed to the front of the court office as the chief flung open the door and exclaimed, "Jerry Lester hung himself in his jail cell with his shoe strings! We cut him down. Thank God, he is not dead yet!"

With that, the red-faced chief collapsed, struck down with a massive heart attack. The clerk immediately called the Johnson Funeral Home across the street to send the ambulance and several good men as the chief was a large man, and they were on the third floor of the courthouse. Frank unbuttoned the gold buttons of the uniform, and they took off the heavy gun belt, loosened his tie and attempted to make him comfortable. They heard another siren, and they could see the town's other ambulance from Wire Funeral Home arriving at the jail to pick up Jerry Lester. He was transported to the hospital where he was found to be barely alive in a brain-dead coma.

The chief was carried down the three flights of marble stairs and sent to the hospital. It was determined he had suffered a massive heart attack, and if he survived at all, it would be many months before he would be able to return to work. Mayor Hutchens appointed Billy Parker as acting chief until Zeno Moore recovered enough to return to duty. The doctor in charge doubted it would ever happen. He was in serious condition.

Jerry Lester was in a coma, brain dead from lack of oxygen due to the hanging attempt. He was kept in the constant care unit with an armed guard at the door. The cost to the county for the room alone was almost ten dollars a day. The county commissioners held an emergency meeting and determined the county could not afford to keep Jerry Lester because of the terrible cost to the taxpayers. They asked the judge to ship Jerry Lester to Michigan City as soon as possible. The judge sent a letter to the warden at the prison about the problem, and the warden replied to the court stating the State Prison would accept Jerry Lester when he could walk in the front door under his own power.

Until then, he was the responsibility of Wabash County, and next time they should keep better watch over their prisoners. Each commissioner said a secret prayer hoping Jerry Lester would die soon to end the county's financial strain. In all the excitement of the murder, the apprehension of the suspect, the trial and the near death of both the convicted man and the police chief, the judge's application to join the Elks had been forgotten.

The Gun from Dooley's Desk

Chapter 7

A MONTH AFTER THE NEWS of the trial and the conviction quieted down, a stranger appeared in Wabash. He checked into the Indiana Hotel and then walked to the Rock City Restaurant for breakfast. Acting Chief Billy Parker was there in his uniform, and soon the two were having a conversation about the recent crime. The man ordered a large breakfast for both men and asked many questions while they ate. By the time they had finished the pot of coffee at the table, Billy thought the man was a reporter for the "Police Gazette," a monthly paper that carried stories about murder and mayhem. Billy hoped he would get paid for telling his story about the murder, the arrest of Jerry Lester and his later conviction. He told it all, often enlarging the importance of his role in the affair.

The man introduced himself as Mr. Allen Burton, Agent, Pinkerton Detective Agency, Indianapolis, Indiana.

He said to Parker, "I'm glad to meet an officer who had such an important part in this case, and I will get back to you later for more details."

Billy was really impressed! Heading back to the office he thought, *Imagine a real Pinkerton detective right here in Wabash! And I had breakfast with him. Wow—Wait till I tell Mom!*

The Gun from Dooley's Desk

Later that morning, the man appeared at the clerk's office and asked to see the official transcripts of the Lester trial and any other records pertaining to the trial. The clerk said he needed the judge's permission to open the records and took the man to the judge's office.

"May I see some identification, please?" Judge McCowen asked. "I am also curious about your interest in this trial."

The man produced his card. "Allen P. Burton, Agent, Pinkerton Detective Agency, Indianapolis, Indiana." The Pinkerton Agency was the largest and best private detective agency in the world and had a reputation for being the best crime solving agency in the country. They charged on a daily basis, and they did not come cheap. The judge was startled; he knew this was something important. *Why is he here? What is he looking for?*

Burton informed the two men the agency had been hired to gather facts about the murder: the arrest and conviction of Jerry Lester, how he apparently hanged himself and the fact that he was now brain dead.

"How did all this happen?" he questioned.

Clerk Miller asked, "Why would anyone be interested in a drifter like Jerry Lester and be willing to pay big bucks to get the information. Who cares about some bum?"

Mr. Burton shocked them when he announced, "My client is Les Lang, from Hollywood, California."

The judge and the clerk were stunned! Les Lang was perhaps the most famous man in Hollywood. Everyone knew the story of Les Lang—the original cowboy movie star who made a hundred one-reel silent movies before moving into the big time. He was riding the crest of fame when the "talkies" came in, but he was not able to make the transition to the new talkie movies. Lang became a director and producer and produced many of the big hits in the late twenties, building a major film studio with many top stars under contract. He sold his studio for ten million dollars cash just before the 1929 crash.

During the Depression, he was flush with cash, so he purchased the real estate that the big studios were located on and then leased it back to them at a huge profit. Lang bought downtown Hollywood land at tax auctions and valley farms at foreclosure sales. By the mid-thirties, he was the wealthiest man in Hollywood and a power base in west coast politics. The governor and senators all sought his attention and friendship. His home was the scene of many parties with famous stars, politicians, bankers, and other influential people as guests. Why would such a man have any interest in a small time attempted robbery and murder in Wabash, Indiana, twenty-five hundred miles from California?

The court clerk Bob Miller provided the transcripts and records for Mr. Burton's inspection. He sat at the large oak table in the clerk's office, carefully reading the handwritten notes and the typewritten records. The only physical evidence, the gun, was locked in the evidence room at the jail. Burton studied the trial records, page by page, making notes of certain items. After several hours, he asked if he could get answers to some questions. The judge had left the office, so it was agreed that the judge, the clerk, and the prosecuting attorney would meet in the morning for an hour to answer any questions.

The Gun from Dooley's Desk

The next day, they sat at the table each with a cup of the clerk's black coffee. Burton had a small list of questions about the trial. He was interested why Morris, the only eyewitness, was not called upon to identify Lester.

Frank Plum answered. "Morris did not see their faces. He saw only their backs as they walked to the rear of the Russell's backyard."

He questioned why the other man at the murder scene had not been identified and charged.

"After much search, the other man was not identified. Perhaps it was a hobo not known to Lester, someone who just rode in on the train that afternoon," Frank said.

Burton asked about the gun. "How was it connected to Lester?"

"We know from the serial number on the gun that it was Dooley's, stolen from his office desk. Mr. Dooley testified that Lester had stayed in his backyard shed for several days last fall. Lester had an opportunity to steal the gun at that time. Mr. Dooley did not know the gun was missing until he saw it in the paper. The kid that found it in the bushes behind the church wiped it clean with an oily rag. Any fingerprints were destroyed," Frank replied.

Burton noted there was not much physical evidence presented at the trial.

"We didn't need a lot of physical evidence. We had an airtight confession, dictated by Lester, written by Chief Moore, witnessed by Officer Parker and signed by Jerry Lester. That was enough to convince the jury of his guilt," Frank said.

Burton was interested in that statement. "Didn't Lester recant the confession before the trial?"

"Not until an attorney was appointed to defend him. Any defense attorney worth his salt would do the same. It's standard procedure, recant the confession. But we have a tight confession, dictated, signed and witnessed by two sworn law officers. It is above reproach, airtight and witnessed by solid persons. We based the case on the confession, and the jury convicted him on the confession. It's solid as a rock," Frank insisted.

"I understand Lester's condition is critical. Will he ever be able to answer any questions?" Burton asked.

The clerk shook his head. "No, he is unconscious, unable to speak. The doctor says he is brain dead. They don't know how long he will live."

Burton thanked the men for their time and walked back to the hotel. As he walked across the lawn, he looked at the courthouse. *What a beautiful stately building, so majestic—but the secrets it hides—no one will ever know!*

. . .

After everyone left the office, Judge McCowen put in a long-distance phone call to his brother Tom in Erie Point.

"Tom, do me a favor. Find out any connection between Les Lang of Hollywood and Jerry Lester of Peru, Indiana." The judge knew they both had circus backgrounds and thought perhaps through Tom's circus printing connection, he could learn something about the two men. Although they were entirely different men with many years apart in age, they could have some family

The Gun from Dooley's Desk

relationship which would explain Les Lang's interest in the trial.

It took Tom just two days to get his brother's requested information. He drove to the judge's office because the telephone in Erie Point was a party line and people could and did listen in. Tom reported that he had gone to Peru to visit his friends that purchase the circus advertising, and within few hours he discovered the connection between Les Lang and Jerry Lester. Lang's real name was Albert Dalton Lester, now 70 years old. He was born and raised in a circus family in Peru, Indiana. He traveled with the family acts, and after he grew up, he ran away from the circus, which was different as most boys ran away to join the circus. He drifted to Hollywood in the early 1920s and got a job in the movies. Because he could ride a horse, he got a part in a western movie, and because he could ride a horse at a gallop, he became a cowboy star.

In Hollywood, he changed his name to Les Lang, wore a big white hat and became America's most famous cowboy. Later, he became a wealthy producer and landowner, but he still kept in contact with his relatives back in Peru. He was an uncle of Jerry Lester's father, and his youngest sister still lived in the Peru area. She had mailed him news clippings about his relatives and sent him a long letter about the family each Christmas. He was far away but not out of touch. Lang learned of the conviction of Jerry Lester and now wanted all the facts. He could afford the best, and the Pinkertons were the best.

"That is why Allen P. Burton is in Wabash asking questions and seeking answers," remarked the judge. The judge took this news and kept it under his hat. There was no reason for everyone in town to know all the facts that he knew. The judge and Tom visited for several hours that evening. Tom told of John Russell coming to the printing office and spending a pleasant afternoon talking, telling stories about old times and killing a bottle of whiskey. It seemed strange that several days later, he was murdered by some bum with a gun.

. . .

At the same time, Burton was a busy man. He went to the hospital to talk to the doctor on duty when Lester was brought to the care room, to the Moore home to talk with the chief on several short visits and to the jail to see the cell where Lester was held. He made a visit to the Russell home and wanted to talk to Mrs. Russell, but she ordered him off the premises. He did get to look at the shooting scene, and he walked down the alley accompanied by Jimmy Johnson who pointed to the exact spot where he found the gun.

Jimmy explained in great detail about finding the gun, the four loaded cartridges, and the one empty shell. Detective Burton gave him one of his business cards. "Allen P. Burton, Agent, Pinkerton Detective Agency, Indianapolis, Indiana." That made Jimmy proud as a peacock. He carried it with him and showed it to everyone including all his customers on the paper route. Later, he stuck it in the frame of the mirror on his dresser in his bedroom; it was his most prized possession, more important than his Little Orphan Annie decoder ring.

The Gun from Dooley's Desk

Burton took the morning Interurban train to Erie Point to visit with Charley Dooley, but Charley did not add anything that was not in the trial. He did show Burton the back office at Dooley's, the box where the gun was kept and the oak roll top desk where the box was stored. Burton asked why the box of cartridges kept in the same box as the gun was not stolen with the gun. It was a full box of fifty with only five removed, those that were in the loaded gun. It seemed strange that someone would steal the gun but leave a full box of shells behind. Charley said Lester was not too bright, or maybe somebody surprised him, and he only had time to steal the gun. Whatever—the gun was gone, and the box of .38 caliber cartridges was still there.

"It was unusual that the first time in several years that John Russell had been in Dooley's Bar was just a few days before he was murdered. Russell came to lunch with Tom McCowen, from the print shop and paper, but much of the lunch was talk and whiskey," Charley confided to Burton.

Allen Burton investigated the shed behind Dooley's where the drifters slept and walked over to the print shop to visit with Thomas, but the shade was down with the "CLOSED" sign on it. As he walked back toward the Interurban station, he passed the beautiful old Catholic church and stopped in to see it and offer a prayer.

Apparently, the first church on this site was a wooden structure built in 1836. An addition was added some five years later, but the growing town soon made it too small. Over time, a fund was established and when $20,000.00 was raised, the building started.

The red brick structure was built in 1870, and the original bell was still in use. The bricks were fired in Huntington and hauled to Erie Point by dray wagons. This was an early time in the settlement. The interior altars and statues were all hand carved. Exquisite stained-glass windows were brought from the east Ohio glassworks. The curved stairs were hand carved native walnut. The front double entry doors were massive and beautifully carved. This noble structure had served the Catholic community well for many years and remained an impressive building.

As he was leaving, he encountered a very attractive lady also leaving the church office. He introduced himself as Mr. Burton from Indianapolis and told her the old church attracted him, so he stopped for a visit. They stood in front of the office by the iron fence. She introduced herself as Mrs. McCowen, a volunteer at the church.

Mr. Burton was surprised and stammered, "I just met a Judge McCowen in Wabash. Are you related?"

"The judge is my husband, and I am glad a stranger from far away is impressed by the old church. It will be 100 years old next year." She smiled, turned and walked away.

Burton took the next Interurban back to Wabash. The next day, he called on the editor of the paper seeking any scraps of information that could have caused someone other than Jerry Lester to have a reason to kill John Russell. It seemed strange someone would shoot the victim in the face; that was more an act of revenge than an act of desperation from a foiled burglar. Editor Perry

The Gun from Dooley's Desk

could not or would not add any new information. When Mrs. Russell, who was now the paper's publisher, was informed the detective was there asking questions, he was ordered to leave and not come back.

Burton talked to many people around town, and while he found John Russell was not the most popular man in town, no one seemed to have any reason to kill him. It was not until he was visiting Prosecutor Frank Plum that the issue of the missing elk's tooth was ever brought up.

"This was not mentioned at the trial nor included in any of the trial records or the police report. We just kept it a secret," Frank said.

The tooth had never been found. The thin gold chain that held it onto the heavy gold watch chain had been broken. No one knew if it had been stolen at the time of the shooting, been lost at the funeral home or if it was not with him that day. Perhaps it was lost days earlier. Jerry Lester did not have it with him, and he had not sold it nor traded it for booze. Burton made a note of the elk's tooth in his report. He did not know if it fit anyplace, but it was one of those odd things. Odd things sometimes turned out to be clues to an inquisitive detective, or sometimes they just cluttered up the case.

He spoke again with Billy Parker and Morris about the missing elk's tooth and what Morris had seen of the two men walking down the back drive that day. Billy was certain the tooth was not on the watch chain nor did he see it when the body was examined at the funeral home later that day. Morris could not remember the tooth on the body although the body was lying face up and the suit coat was open. He remembered seeing the watch chain draped across the vest but nothing else.

During this conversation, Morris said he noticed that the two men walking back down the drive that day were different in stature. One was chunky, one was skinny, and both wore old clothes. The skinny one carried the cloth bag and walked funny. Jerry Lester was a skinny man, but at the trial, Morris was not asked to identify Jerry Lester as one of the men he saw in the Russell yard that day. Burton found it interesting that the only witness who saw the two hobos leaving the yard was not asked to identify the suspect at the jail or during the trial.

"I did not see the faces of the hobos. I could not positively identify Jerry Lester, so they did not call me to testify at the trial. The signed confession was enough for the jury to convict," Morris admitted.

While Burton was talking to Morris in the alley behind the Russell home, Garl Coleman drove down the alley toward his house a few doors down. He observed the notebook in Burton's hand with interest and the notes he was making while interviewing Morris. It caused him much concern. He wished this were all over and the town could return to its normal life with his secret kept safe. He had no way of knowing whether Russell had taken notes while he was checking at the Huntington hospital and the courthouse, but nothing had been mentioned about finding one. If such a reporter's notebook existed, a man like Burton would find it. That would be very bad for the Colemans. Garl wished this would all just go away.

The Gun from Dooley's Desk

Chapter 8

THE COUNTY COMMISSIONERS met at their monthly meeting to ask for more money for their budget, as the cost of keeping Jerry Lester at the local hospital was very expensive. There was no provision at the jail to keep him, and the doctor required him to have twenty-four-hour oxygen and a feeding tube to keep him alive. The doctor could not tell them when, if ever, he was going to get better, but he did not get worse. The police had already removed the twenty-four-hour guard from his hospital room. He was in a coma and was not going to escape.

Allen Burton wanted to talk to some of Russell's friends while he was in Wabash and called several. All spoke to him but could add very little information. He met with Garl Coleman at the Elks Lodge. Over lunch, Garl spoke of his friend Russell, how important a man he was in the community but added little information. Later, Burton asked to meet with Coleman again to go over some little things that were unanswered. Coleman agreed to meet him at his office the next day. When Burton arrived at the factory, there was a group of men standing outside the gate. Burton could tell something was wrong. Coleman invited him into his office, and Burton asked about the men outside the fence.

The Gun from Dooley's Desk

"Today, we had to lay off most of the plant workers due to the lack of orders. They did not know until the start of the workday, and it made them very angry."

Coleman was clearly upset, and Burton could tell he was under extreme pressure, but he answered his questions.

Coleman stated, "I am convinced the murderer was convicted. It was a terrible thing for a well-respected citizen like John Russell to be murdered in his own yard and nothing taken but his elk's tooth."

This came like a bolt of lightning to Burton! The tooth had not been included in the police report nor the trial. Why had Coleman specifically stated the elk's tooth was stolen? No one knew that except the hobos. After the interview, Burton went back to the police station and again visited with acting chief Big Billy Parker. Burton asked the chief if anyone knew about the missing elk's tooth.

Billy said only the robbers would know. It was not listed in the police report on purpose. They were hoping to use it as a means of identification when the killers were found. In fact, it did not seem important at the time. Then Burton knew that Coleman had more information to give. He phoned Coleman's home and asked to see him.

"I will not talk to you again. I am very busy with the business and have met you twice. Enough is enough. Go away." Garl knew the detective had learned something about the murder and would be around asking questions until it was solved.

Garl Coleman's world was collapsing about his head. His factory was bankrupt, his home was mortgaged to the hilt, and his whole life was a lie. It was possible that he would be exposed as a child molester and the father of an illegitimate child. Garl had several whiskeys on ice and later just straight whiskey before he picked up the telephone and made a long-distance call. When there was an answer on the other end, Coleman was very distraught and cried out that something was up. The detective knew something and kept coming back with more questions. His business had failed that day, and the bank would be calling tomorrow about the past due payments. He rambled on, saying he wished they had never met, and as he got more drunk, he became very depressed. Finally, he hung up.

Garl announced to his wife that he was going to the Elks and would be late returning. When he had not returned by eleven o'clock, his wife called the Elks, but the bartender said they had not seen him all evening. When Mrs. Coleman went to the garage to see if his car was there, she found him. The car was running with a hose from the exhaust pipe going into the vehicle. Sitting in the driver's seat was Garl Coleman—now very dead.

Big Billy Parker was present when the coroner and an assistant from the funeral home removed Garl Coleman's body. It was apparent the death was a suicide by carbon monoxide; no evidence of foul play was present. No note was found on the body, in the car or the house. Coleman had apparently left the house, gone to the factory, collected the hose, driven back home and connected the hose to the exhaust pipe. It was a normal suicide. Reverend Warner, the minister from their church, came to the house that night to console the wife and daughter.

The Gun from Dooley's Desk

The following morning, several women from the church as well as the minister came to the house to help with the arrangements.

Mrs. Coleman called the paper and gave them the information for the obituary. She said Garl Coleman was a well-loved Christian man who dedicated his life to his family, his church, and his community. He was especially proud of his service to the Elks Lodge and the time he put in serving that fine institution. Garl was a trustee of his church and devoted much time and money for its growth. His devotion to his family was well known, and he was especially proud of his daughter Lucille Coleman.

A large church funeral was planned, and the owner of the funeral home said it was the most expensive casket they had ever sold. The city would miss Garl Coleman, a substantial citizen and a community leader. Nothing was stated in the obituary about the cause of death, but soon the town was buzzing with stories and rumors of the suicide and why it took place.

The church was packed. There were so many floral arrangements, every available space was filled. Beautiful flowers decorated the entrance, were displayed throughout the nave and adorned the altar. The minister went on about the dearly departed. He was a great citizen, a church deacon, a community leader and family man.

"Garl Coleman was a man we should all admire for his contribution to mankind in his lifetime of work," Reverend Warner declared with reverence.

His wife and daughter sobbed, his friends wiped away the tears, and all in all, it was a grand funeral. The body was taken in Johnson Funeral Home's new Ford hearse to Falls Avenue Cemetery, and after a tearful graveside service, he was laid to rest. The large red granite headstone was placed, suitable for a man of his great importance—so ended the life of Garl Coleman.

Two weeks after the funeral, the City Bank quietly moved in a manager to run the factory as assistant to Sarah Coleman and to get the plant running again. The manager, a middle-aged man, named Oliver Pezzell, had successfully managed a sizeable family-owned church furniture factory for several years. After the death of one of the founders, the heirs split over control. A family member took charge and Oliver was let go. City Bank held a large mortgage on the Coleman factory for the plant expansion and all the new machines and equipment. The bank needed to find an experienced manager to save the company and protect their loan.

Oliver Pezzell was the result of their search. University educated, business trained and experienced in wood manufacturing were the factors in his success in saving the Coleman company during the depression and later significantly expanding the cabinet manufacturing business. Oliver was in complete control of the company and within a year had taken the place of Garl in the Coleman bed, much to Sarah Coleman's satisfaction.

Oliver purchased the beautiful brick colonial home on West Hill Street from the Bates Estate, and some folks wondered why a bachelor would need such a large family home. He contracted workers to repair, paint and polish until it was again a stately showplace. Oliver employed a part time housekeeper to cook and clean; her son kept the yard and exterior neatly trimmed. The large home was

The Gun from Dooley's Desk

next door to the impressive Women's Clubhouse. Both properties bordered the beautiful city park. It was a typical West Hill Street home, where the upper-class residents held forth.

. . .

The day after the funeral, Billy Parker phoned the Wabash Inn where Allen Burton was staying and suggested they meet for breakfast the next morning at the Rock City Café. Over sausage and eggs with lots of hot coffee, Billy Parker confided to Burton that he had found a suicide note when he searched Garl Coleman's office at the factory. The note was in Coleman's private office on his desk, written on a Coleman company letterhead with Garl's blue fountain pen alongside. Parker did not want anyone in the police department to know about this new development, but he did trust and respect Burton, a professional detective. After breakfast, they sat in the black Plymouth police car, parked in the fireman's parking lot while Burton read and reread the note.

To my family,

My life is over. A secret from my past, which I deplore, is about to be exposed to the world. My reputation will be ruined, my family shamed and my daughter's life devastated. John Russell was the cause of it all. He was an evil man, willing and eager to expose this horrible story that happened years ago. That's why it was necessary for us to kill him. He deserved to die, to stop the blackmail of innocent people, to stop the pain and suffering he was about to unleash. It is not our fault. It was he who caused his own death.

We did it to protect our families, not ourselves. May God forgive us for what we have done, and may God welcome me, as I have been a follower of our Lord. Goodbye, dear wife, we will be together again in heaven. Goodbye Lucille, you have your life ahead of you now. No one can ruin it for you. I love you, and I did it for you. For my partner in this act, you can now rest knowing your secrets are safe, for only I know, and now I cannot tell.

Goodbye and may God forgive us,
Garl Coleman

The Gun from Dooley's Desk

Burton gasped in surprise. His mind raced. *Russell shot by Coleman! Why, why, why? What did Russell have on Coleman that was so significant, it would drive a man to murder? And the big question, who is the "we" he wrote about? There were two people at the murder site according to Morris, the only witness who saw the killers. If Coleman was one, who was the other? What kind of motive did the second person have to hate Russell enough to be a part of a murder plot? How did Coleman get the gun from Dooley's? He had never been in the place. Did he buy it from some hobo who had stolen it from Dooley's?*

How did two people shoot a man in cold blood in the light of the afternoon and not have anyone see them clearly? Morris said they looked like hobos. Were they disguised—and if they were—did they hide the disguises at the Coleman garage? It was east of the Russell house, so they could have walked east in the alley to the car parked at Coleman's garage. Why throw the gun in the bushes behind the church? They would know it would be found in time.

Many questions went through his mind, but the answers did not follow. With this astounding information, it was clear that Burton's work was completed. He had been hired to find the facts about Jerry Lester and the crime. It was now apparent that Jerry Lester had nothing to do with the murder. He was an innocent man and although innocent, was nearly dead. What legal action would follow was not a decision Burton had to make. His job was to get the facts, and now he had them—his job was done.

Billy Parker was almost in tears. He could see a huge scandal brewing. Here was an innocent man in the hospital nearly dead, who was unjustly charged. Lester was convicted by a false confession he helped write after he and the chief almost beat Lester to death. Billy knew that Les Lang had the power and money to carry this to court, and when the facts came out, Billy would be charged with a crime. If Lester died, he and the chief could be charged with murder. Neither he nor his family had the money to hire a lawyer, and he was sure the city would not provide one. Besides, he would be fired immediately and would lose all the power and attention he was now getting.

Something had to be done, and the only man in this town he could trust was sitting in the car with him. He had to convince Allen Burton to help him find the second killer, so he could bring this scandal to an end before it leaked out. Billy surmised that Burton was not interested in spending more time on this case, especially if he were not getting paid. Billy had an angle, which would get them both some money, and he related the plan to Burton. If Burton would help and they solved this crime, Billy would sell the story to the Police Gazette or some other crime magazine and split the money with Burton. This would get Billy back in the good graces of the city's mayor and city council. Hopefully, he would then be appointed the City of Wabash Chief of Police.

Burton said he would think about the deal that night and give Billy his answer in the morning. Later back at the hotel, Burton studied all the known facts of the case. First, Jerry Lester was not involved. He was just in the wrong place at the wrong time and was a lowlife bum. Second, Garl Coleman was one of the two people that did the killing, and the second person was unknown. It was not known which person fired the fatal shot.

The Gun from Dooley's Desk

Third, John Russell had discovered something that was important enough about Coleman and the other person; it got him murdered. Russell had found this out just recently because Coleman's note indicated it was about to happen. Fourth, the gun was stolen from Dooley's bar in Erie Point. Coleman had no known connection with Erie Point, so the second person was connected in some way. Fifth, the elk's tooth emblem was important enough to the killers to take it from the body either during the shooting or after when the body was lying in the flower bed. It had not shown up; it may or may not be a clue.

Burton studied the facts and concluded that once his report was filed stating that Jerry Lester was an innocent victim, the scandal would be in the open. He was certain the widow of Russell would use every power of the local press to uncover the facts, and the suicide note of Coleman's would bring down the entire city government.

While Burton was reflecting on these disconnected facts, the hotel desk clerk called his room.

"The night policeman just stopped in and informed me that Jerry Lester has died in the local hospital," he said.

Now the fat was in the fire. Soon, Billy Parker called on the phone to tell Burton the latest news. He started talking about the deal they could have together when Burton told him to shut up. (He knew that the hotel desk clerk sat at the switchboard and listened in on the hotel phone calls and was probably listening to this one.) Parker said to meet him for breakfast at the Rock City in the morning.

At breakfast, Parker was a nervous wreck. He did not sleep that night. He was positive if the word got out about Coleman, or if Coleman had told anyone else, he and Chief Moore would be charged with conspiracy to commit murder, because of the false confession they had prepared and forced Lester to sign. Both committed perjury by giving false testimony in court and lying about Lester's attempt to escape—it didn't happen. When returning from Peru, they had stopped in a secluded place and beat him badly enough to require a trip to the hospital before going to jail. Parker was terrified and did not know what to do. He told Burton he had burned the suicide note.

That afternoon at the jail office, Billy Parker studied the Coleman suicide note and reflected on what great harm this little piece of paper could cause him. He could be fired, arrested, charged with a serious crime and stand trial. He realized he could be found guilty and serve a prison sentence. All this brought on by this one-page note. He had a strong impulse to burn it, especially since he told Burton he had destroyed it, but it was evidence in a murder case. Destroying evidence, he had taken an oath to protect was a reflection on his honor, not what he wanted to do.

He needed to protect himself without violating his honor. He would hide it away in a secure place, where he could reclaim it, but others would not look. Suddenly, the perfect hiding place came to mind. *That's where it will go. Without the note, I cannot be connected with the Lester arrest, trial, or his death.* Parker felt relieved—at last, he was now safe. *No one will ever know.*

The Gun from Dooley's Desk

Back at the hotel, Allen Burton decided to end this investigation and leave town. He was afraid that Parker was an unstable person and if caught in a corner would be capable of doing bad things, even murder. Burton checked out of the hotel and walked to the Interurban station. Before catching the westbound to Peru, he called the police station from the pay phone. Billy Parker was not there, but the desk officer took the message. Burton reported his investigation was completed, he was leaving that day and would not ever return to Wabash. On the train, he felt relieved to be away from this town. It had looked so peaceful when he arrived. Now he knew the dark secrets swirling within the city, and they were not pretty.

Chapter 9

BACK IN HIS INDIANAPOLIS OFFICE, Allen Burton carefully prepared his written report, the facts developed about the Jerry Lester case in Wabash. It was then submitted to the chief inspector before being typed up and mailed to the client Les Lang, in Hollywood. Allen very carefully outlined the investigation. He started with the known facts of the Russell murder, the arrest of Jerry Lester, the circumstantial evidence against him, the critical signed confession, his renouncing the confession, the trial, the jury's verdict, the attempted suicide and finally his death in the hospital.

There were too many loose facts. Morris, the only eyewitness, did not testify at the trial. Lester was never identified at the site, there was no robbery attempt, and nothing was stolen. There was no evidence connecting Lester to the gun and no proof Dooley's gun was the murder weapon. Dooley's gun was stolen, but there was no evidence Lester took it a year earlier.

There was no apparent motive for the murder. The second person was never identified nor located after an extensive search. It was unknown who fired the killing bullet. It could have been fired by the second unknown person. The kid that found the gun wiped it clean; there were no fingerprints to trace.

The Gun from Dooley's Desk

No, the evidence was full of holes, and there was only one thing solid. The jury convicted Lester on the strength of that confession—it was airtight. Allen wrote that he doubted Lester was guilty of the murder. He closed his report by stating he was sorry about Jerry Lester, and while he was a well-known petty thief, it was not proven he was the perpetrator of this heinous murder. Jerry Lester was an easy target. He suffered from the bumbling of the police investigation—not an unheard-of act in the depression days of the 1930s. In his final statement, Burton suggested Jerry Lester was an innocent victim of police corruption, false evidence, and questionable testimony. He was wrongly convicted by a system eager to get a guilty verdict. But now he was dead, a sorry miscarriage of justice.

This concluded his report. His contract was to get the information on the Lester trial, which he did. He carefully omitted that he had seen a suicide note from Garl Coleman confessing to the murder. *No, some things are best left unsaid. Besides, the note has been destroyed.* The large brown envelope with the PINKERTON AGENCY logo containing the final report was mailed to Hollywood, another investigation completed. Allen Burton was sent to another case, a theft from an Express Office in Madison County, Indiana.

• • •

The Hollywood studio office received a legal size manila envelope marked for Mr. Lang, "PERSONAL," from The Pinkerton Agency. The secretary placed it on his desk. Les had been out of the office for several days, and he was returning from a studio function accompanied by several of his writers, a director, and one of his producers. They planned to have a production meeting that afternoon. While waiting for others to arrive, they visited and kidded around. Les scanned the mail on his desk, spotted the Pinkerton report, opened it and carefully read it. Without a word, he handed it to the others to read.

The men gathered around the table, studied the report and discussed the contents—the tragedy of it all, how an innocent man suffered and died because he was poor. They all agreed there could be an appealing story here, a powerful movie about exploited people with no one to protect them. An ambitious prosecutor and an incompetent police department made this possible, and a real tragic film story was in this report.

One writer voiced a different thought. "Who is the real killer, and what was the motive to kill a local small-town newspaper editor? Simple robbery or something more sinister? The editor might be the story; he might be screwing some hot babe with a jealous husband, or he wrote something that pissed someone off. The hobo's just the one that got caught. This editor may not be the most popular person in town."

The producer stood up. "Get me a good script, and I will produce it."

The writers all agreed there was a great story there. Les was pacing the floor and thinking out loud. "Who could we get for the leading man? Maybe Tyrone Powers."

Writer Sam Jacobs noted the event happened in Wabash, Indiana. He recalled his roommate at Indiana

The Gun from Dooley's Desk

University had graduated in the new Law Enforcement School and was an Indiana State Police Officer, presently stationed in Wabash. Sam and Michael McCaffery had kept in touch with occasional letters and an annual Christmas note, catching up on the year's events. Perhaps he could be of help in this search. Sam told the others and made a suggestion.

"I'll send him a letter asking for his help. He will find it exciting to have a connection in Hollywood."

They all agreed Sam should make that contact with his college buddy. Having a friend in official places was a good idea. Les Lang was always a man to grasp every opportunity and gave instructions to his secretary.

"Send a letter off to Pinkerton's Indianapolis office. Get that agent Burton to go back to Wabash soon and find the actual killers of the editor as well as the motive behind it all. The studio will pick up all the costs, per diem plus expenses—get moving—a new movie could be produced from the results. The movie could be a blockbuster, a box office smash hit and perhaps an Academy Award winner!"

. . .

As these events were unfolding in Hollywood, back in Indiana things took a new twist. Lucille Coleman was driving her blue 1935 Ford convertible coupe back from a shopping trip in Fort Wayne one afternoon. On US 24 east of Andrews, she passed a slow-moving truck on a hill. This was observed by a state policeman traveling well behind her. He used the siren to pull her over, asked for her license, and gave her a verbal warning about no-passing zones. He wrote her a ticket for passing in a restricted zone. She would have to appear in the J.P. Traffic Court in Wabash and pay the fine. When he examined her license, he recognized her name and remembered they both attended Manchester College even had several classes together.

"Lucille? What a shock! I didn't recognize you at first. We went to college together. I'm Michael McCaffery. Do you remember me?"

"Why, yes! Goodness, it *is* you."

He recalled with some pleasure when they both attended a Halloween hayride and costume party. She came dressed as Cinderella. He came dressed as Abraham Lincoln, beard, top hat and all. Because Manchester was a strict Baptist college, and no dancing was allowed on the campus, the party was held at the Lukens Lake Pavilion. Shorty Washburn and his four-piece band entertained, and all danced under the bright autumn moon overlooking beautiful Lukens Lake. While there was no dating, they did happen to dance together several times.

Lucille remembered Michael McCaffery, the good-looking young Irish guy, not a great dancer but a smooth talker who tried unsuccessfully to get a date with her. Dating was not allowed on the campus, but many students found ways to get around the rules. This young lad was eager to get her to go to the local movie with him, but she declined. Now she wished she had because even though they were college chums together and she suggested he just give her a warning citation, he still gave her a three-dollar traffic ticket.

The Gun from Dooley's Desk

Lucille was very impressed with this good-looking, well-mannered young man in his starched and pressed blue and gray state police uniform. She offered an invitation to call on her Sunday afternoon when her mother would be home.

"Would you like to come by and have a Coke or a cup of coffee? We could catch up on the events since college days, your career with the new Indiana State Police and my new position teaching music in all five elementary Wabash City schools."

He answered quickly. "It will be great fun catching up on all that has happened. If you give me your address, I will see you then."

The following Sunday, her mother was also impressed with the polite young man even though he was Irish and from Erie Point.

In the next few months, Michael and Lucille were seen together attending the Saturday night movies at the Eagles Theater, enjoying a Coke at the Sweet Shop and other events about town. They always drove her car because his only auto was the black Indiana State Police car that was parked in his garage ready to respond to a duty call.

When Michael McCaffery went to Dick's Men's Wear to purchase his first black tuxedo, everyone learned he would accompany Lucille Coleman, the most eligible young lady in town, to the Women's Club Annual Ball. The biggest social event in Wabash each year was the Annual Ball held at the stately Women's Clubhouse joining the city park. A big-name band came down from Chicago, and the cream of Wabash society as well as those who wish they were, attended. Strict dress rules prevailed: black tux for men and long evening gowns for ladies.

For most men in Wabash, this was the only time each year the tux was taken out of the bag and hung on the outdoor clothesline to air out the mothball smell. The Beitman & Wolf Department Store sold several new gowns for the gala event. It was the one bright spot in the grim depression days—when polite society celebrated—forgetting for a moment the dark days at hand. The local, young unmarried girls were all eager to get a date for the event just like the senior prom, except it was for grownups.

It had been nearly a year since the death of her father, and Sarah Coleman gave Lucille permission to attend the ball. The beautiful Lucille Coleman, escorted by handsome young Michael McCaffery, the Irish lad from Erie Point, was the center of attention. Wabash society would never be the same again—a young Irish Mick with the town's most eligible young lady. Lucille and Michael had a thrilling evening, perhaps the perfect couple. The future was brighter that night.

Sarah Coleman was one of the club officers and dressed in a very formal gown. Some noted that Oliver Pezzell danced with her several times including the last dance of the evening. Oliver was a well-mannered, good-looking middle-aged man, in a tailored tux and well versed in the social graces. His connection with the local bank was well known, but his attention to the recent widow was noticed for the first time. The Women's Club Annual Ball was a smashing success! The Wabash Daily News carried a three column write up about the event with pictures. All present were named, and all that attended saved that paper in their scrapbooks. "The Grand Event of the Year," society's bright light shone even in the darkest days of the depression.

Sarah Coleman now owned the Coleman Cabinet & Fine Furniture Factory. Oliver was her lover, friend, and manager. For several months, they worked together well and had many things in common. Soon, Oliver was escorting Sarah to the Sunday service at the Presbyterian church where he taught a youth Bible Study class, and Sarah sang in the choir. It was not a surprise to anyone when the society page of the newspaper carried a formal announcement of their engagement and coming marriage.

Chapter 10

IN INDIANAPOLIS, the Pinkerton office manager was elated they had an open-ended contract with a real Hollywood studio, cost plus expenses. Those contracts were scarce during the hard times of the depression. Allen Burton was back on the road to Wabash with mixed feelings of uncertainty and even a sense of danger. Burton was not sure how to proceed with this investigation. He and Chief Billy Parker were the only people who knew about the Coleman suicide note and the confession. He would have to be very careful. Parker could be a problem when the facts came out—even dangerous.

Michael McCaffery received a letter from his college chum Sam Jacobs, apparently now a big-time studio writer in Hollywood, asking for any assistance he could render in the examination of the Russell murder. A Pinkerton detective named Allen Burton would be returning to Wabash soon to conduct an investigation. Burton would telephone Michael when he arrived to get a local contact—un-officially of course. Michael reflected and remembered a little about the trial: his Uncle Terrance McCowen was the judge, the defendant was a well-known drunk and hobo, and John Russell was the local newspaper editor, murdered during a botched robbery attempt.

The Gun from Dooley's Desk

That was all he could recall about the case. He had not been assigned to Wabash at the time it occurred. As he reread the letter, he said to himself, "A Pinkerton agent—that's costing somebody a lot of money. I wonder what the fuss is all about. Some hobo killing somebody? No, there's more than that, it will be interesting to see what develops." Michael wrote an answer to his friend, congratulating him for getting a writing job with a big-time Hollywood studio. He offered his help with Burton in an unofficial way. "If I came out to Hollywood to visit, could you introduce me to some of those Hollywood starlets pictured in the magazines? Perhaps a good looking Irish lad would make an impression on those Hollywood sweater gals."

. . .

Lucille Coleman had a grave concern about her father's death by suicide and it bothered her. She requested the family law firm Plum & Plum to look into the reason. They suggested it was due to a slow-down in business: few new orders, a substantial loss of money and the layoff of the employees. The family business was in trouble. The expansion a few years earlier created a large bank loan and making those payments was a big problem. She was not impressed with their answer; her father never indicated the situation was as dire as they suggested. Perhaps there was something else? She asked her gentleman friend if he could offer any advice.

"The Pinkerton Agency will have an experienced operator in town for another investigation," Michael said.

"Perhaps he could also look into this."

Burton arrived in Wabash, checked into the Wabash Hotel, unpacked and found a telegram from his office instructing him to contact the Law Office of Plum & Plum. They were the attorneys for the Coleman Estate and would have a retainer check. He was surprised to learn they wanted an investigation of the Coleman suicide. Burton was concerned; only he and Billy Parker knew of the Coleman connection with the Russell murder. *How do I handle this?*

Burton met with Chief Billy Parker that evening and told him he was working on the case of the Coleman suicide and the Russell murder along with the Jerry Lester trial. Parker was terrified because if it were discovered the two cases were connected, he would be in serious trouble. He could be charged with accessory to murder, conspiracy to hide evidence and perjury, and lying under oath in a capital murder trial. Long jail time could be his future. He was terrified at the thought, but his brain could not find a solution to his problem.

Burton started his investigation, beginning at the Coleman office. He interviewed Oliver Pezzell, now the plant manager, as well as the shop superintendent, the office manager, the bookkeeper, and lastly Mrs. Coleman. They could offer little information not already discovered. He borrowed the daily log book to study and asked to see the car that was used in the suicide. It was stored at the City Garage. Mrs. Coleman would not drive it; she was planning to have them sell it later. Under the watchful eye of the manager, Burton uncovered the blue Oldsmobile

The Gun from Dooley's Desk

four-door and examined the interior. Nothing seemed amiss; then he announced his search was over and left.

Burton was concerned. When the truth came out, Parker would be in real trouble and could go to prison for a long stretch. He was not too stable anyway and now could be really dangerous. Burton felt there was no one in town he could trust. He recalled the studio gave him a local name to contact, a local state police officer no less, just the person he needed now. Burton called Michael McCaffery and arranged to meet him that evening at the hotel coffee shop and have some dinner together. "I'll buy," Burton said.

The two men met, got acquainted, chatted about things and seemed to strike it off as friends quickly. They were both professionals, each admired the other's abilities, and above all, they trusted each other. Michael understood the information he would hear was part of an investigation and was very confidential. Michael agreed Parker must know that he was now aware of the facts. Parker should not do anything stupid because a state police officer knew the whole story.

Burton told the story as he knew it: Jerry Lester, the trial, the confession, the conviction, the jailhouse hanging, his death and last, the story of the Coleman suicide note. He also noted that Parker burned the Coleman suicide note to cover his crime against Lester. The note was gone; there was no direct evidence. His conclusion was Coleman and another person killed Russell, and Jerry Lester was innocent of this crime. The motive was still a mystery, and the identity of the other person was unknown.

Michael was concerned after hearing this information and wondered if his position as a law enforcement officer required him to report this to his superiors. Given the fact that his lady friend's father was deeply involved and had confessed to a major crime, but with no proof as the note was destroyed, he was not sure what his role should be. He was a law enforcement officer, but so far this was unofficial. He loved his job and didn't want to do anything that could jeopardize his position—he must be cautious.

He worried about Lucille. *Does she know anything about this?* Michael and Lucille had already looked at a diamond engagement ring together, considering a wedding next year. The fact her father had confessed to a brutal murder in a suicide note, now destroyed, was unreal. *What drove Coleman to commit such a crime? What could cause a man to take such a terrible action? What could be the motive? How do I know this story is even true? What should I do now?* Michael explained to Burton that he was confused by all this. He would need to think about what his position should be.

Both agreed this was dangerous stuff and mum was the word. They shook hands, vowed secrecy, agreed Parker should be informed that Officer McCaffery had knowledge of his actions and departed. Burton called Parker from a pay phone in the lobby, so the night clerk could not listen in and informed him of the meeting with Officer McCaffery.

That night, Burton slept with a revolver under his pillow. Michael did not sleep, worrying about it all. Parker spent the night at the fishing shack west of town on the Wabash River, drinking Three Feathers whiskey shots chased by Drewry's beer. His smoky lantern ran out of oil early in the morning, but he had passed out long before. When he didn't show up for duty the next day, the office called his mother and asked if anyone had seen him. She had not. A search was started, and phone calls were made to all his old drinking buddies. He was not with any of them. No one had seen him last night.

The next day, they found his body at the river shack. Apparently, he was cleaning his revolver when it accidentally discharged killing him instantly. The front-page story in the newspaper did not mention the empty whiskey bottle or the case of empty beer bottles on the table and floor. The paper omitted the fact it might have been a self-inflicted gunshot. They called him a good officer who did a decent job as acting police chief. The city would have a day of mourning for him—a black banner on all government offices in the city.

His funeral was about a fallen Officer of the Law, the city's first. The Reverend Warner performed the funeral service, praising Billy for his devotion to the Wabash Police Department. The mayor spoke about this acting chief lost to an unfortunate accident. The police officers in uniform served as pallbearers—all in all—Billy went out in style. His parents mourned the loss of their son, the only wage earner in the home. The future looked dark for the Parkers. The only hero the family ever had, a real police officer, was gone.

Chapter 11

MICHAEL AND HIS MOTHER visited his Aunt Phyllis and Dr. Nagle at Huntington that weekend. During the afternoon, Patty came over to see them. She attended college and worked in the clerk's office, so she didn't get to visit very often. Patty admired her favorite cousin Michael and spent time with him whenever possible. She asked him about his duties as the local state police officer and what exciting crimes he was working on—bank robberies or murders. She mentioned the John Russell murder. Michael replied he was in Indianapolis when the Russell murder occurred, and he didn't know any of the facts except their Uncle Terrance was the presiding judge.

"I met Mr. Russell when he came to look up a record at the Huntington Courthouse," Patty said.

"What kind of record?" Michael asked.

"A birth record that happened over twenty years ago because I had to go back and open the archives to find the actual yearbook he wanted. The name he wanted was O'Dell, the same as Mom's maiden name. Mr. Russell seemed very interested in what he found because he carefully copied it down in his notebook and thanked me for my help." Patty remembered it occurred just a few days before he was murdered. She had never seen him before that day in Huntington.

The Gun from Dooley's Desk

"Could that be a clue?" Patty asked and laughed.

"It seems a bit odd the editor himself would come here for such a little bit of information, but newspaper people look up things and make notes all the time, that's their business," Michael replied. He wondered if anyone had located Russell's notebook and looked at the contents, and he made a mental note to ask Allen Burton about that fact. Phyllis fried some chickens, and they all stayed for dinner that evening. Lydia, Michael, Phyllis, Dr. Nagle, Patty, and her husband enjoyed the evening and their time together.

They talked about family matters, the depression, how bad business was, and their great Democratic President Roosevelt.

"He could solve these problems if given half a chance by Congress and that damned Supreme Court! Those eleven old men are stopping our president from bringing back prosperity to our country. It would happen except for the court," Phyllis remarked.

Lydia was collecting payments for funerals a few dollars at a time. Dr. Nagle was unable to collect many of the office calls he made even when he lowered the visit to two dollars and a hospital baby delivery to thirty dollars. It was hard to collect from people who had no money and no steady jobs.

They kidded Michael about having a government job with a steady income. They were joking, but they were very proud of him. He was one of the first of the new breed of Indiana State Police: professionally trained, college degree, hired because of ability and not politically appointed. This was a new age in the scandal-ridden

Indiana State Police, formerly made up of political hacks, relatives of elected state officials and jobs used as payoffs for political debts. It was an honor to have been selected, and Michael was proud of his role in the new State Police Program. Michael and his mother departed, and he drove her home to Erie Point then returned to Wabash.

Phyllis and Patty chatted in the kitchen finishing the dishes while their husbands listened to WOWO evening news on the radio.

"I told Michael about Mr. Russell coming to the courthouse to look up an item about a girl named O'Dell, who had a baby girl in 1911. You and Dad both signed the birth certificate. He was very interested in the record. Do you suppose it is some kind of a clue?"

Phyllis' heart skipped a beat when she heard that from her daughter, but she calmly answered, "Newspaper people often look up things that happened long ago, that is part of their job."

That night, before they went to bed, Phyllis and her husband had a long and serious talk about Russell discovering their secret. What would it mean? Who could it hurt? Twenty-four years ago, they were positive: *no one will ever know.*

. . .

Allen Burton was very busy the next few days, interviewing many people that had any connection to the Russell murder, the Coleman suicide, or Jerry Lester. He carefully reviewed all the information that others had gathered. Burton did not know how the "accidental"

The Gun from Dooley's Desk

shooting death of Chief Parker would fit into this hodgepodge of fact and fiction, but his fears about Parker were confirmed. He was unstable, and his suicide proved it.

The Wabash Inn Hotel where Burton was staying was owned and managed by Jerry Lynn. The hotel business had been in the Lynn family since the days of the Erie Canal. The family built an inn across the corner from the dock in 1850, and at least one member of the family had operated a hotel business since. In 1928, the family built the present Wabash Inn, an impressive three-story brick building covering a quarter block in the heart of Wabash.

Jerry Lynn was an active Rotary member, and as the Rotary Club met at the hotel every Wednesday noon, Jerry was always on the lookout for speakers for the club's noon program. He learned that the Pinkerton Agency employed Allen Burton, and he asked Burton if he would give a program about the agency at the following Wednesday's luncheon. Burton agreed although he could not mention the case he was working in Wabash. However, he could talk about the agency in general.

Pinkerton was the world's most famous detective agency for nearly a hundred years. Burton gave a program for the Rotary Club that Wednesday, speaking to a full house, all Rotary members and many of their friends. Everyone was interested in hearing about the famous Pinkerton Detective Agency. He received a small plaque given to speakers, a token of appreciation for presenting an exciting program. After the meeting, many members introduced themselves, remarked about the excellent program and thanked him for speaking to the club.

Then an extraordinary thing happened! A Rotary member named Pete Johnson came up to Burton and introduced himself as the owner of the Johnson Funeral Home. Burton had visited the funeral home during the investigation of the Russell murder but had not met him.

"Yesterday, we were cleaning the inside of the van, which is also used as the ambulance. Down in a space behind the seat, I found a notebook. It had fallen out of the upper suit coat pocket of John Russell as his body was being transported to the funeral home," Pete told him in a confidential voice. "The notebook belongs to Mrs. Russell, but we are embarrassed to have mislaid it all this time. Would you like to review it before we tell Mrs. Russell we just recently found it?"

"Yes, I'll pick it up at the funeral home this afternoon." Burton tried to conceal his excitement; clues did not fall in his hands so easily. All it cost was a twenty-minute talk at the Rotary Club.

That night, Burton reviewed the notebook entries carefully, seeking any noticeable entries that might trigger further study. Several items were interesting, but he didn't know what connection if any, they had with the investigation. Because Burton did not know any of the names in the notebook, he called Michael and invited him to join him for dinner at the Hotel Grill. He asked Michael to look at the notebook and see if any of the entries had any meaning to him.

After dinner, Michael studied the notebook page by page. Nothing was noteworthy until he saw the name and phone number of his Uncle Tom McCowen at the Erie Point Free Press. He also noted the number of the court

The Gun from Dooley's Desk

clerk of Huntington County and then several notations. The one that struck him was the notation about the birth of a baby born in 1911, the O'Dell baby. Russell's handwritten entry listed: Mother, Linda O'Dell, age 16; Father, no name listed; Address, Huntington, Indiana; Baby's name, Lucille. Dr. Nagle signed the birth certificate as the delivery doctor, and Phyllis Nagle, RN signed as the delivery nurse. A notation, "private placement."

Michael was astounded by the facts he just read. Could that be his Aunt Linda? Her maiden name was O'Dell, but he had never known much about her life before she married Uncle Terrance. It appeared that many years ago, as a teenager, his Aunt Linda had given birth to a girl child at the Huntington Hospital. Dr. Nagle and Aunt Phyllis did the delivery of the baby girl. Michael could not believe what he had read.

Aunt Linda, the straightest of the straight, giving birth to an illegitimate child when she was 16 years old. What happened to the child, is it somewhere in the family? He had never heard anything about this. Obviously this child had been a well-kept family secret. His mind raced with the thought of it all. *This occurred many years ago. Why bring it up now? Why would Russell be interested in a teenager giving birth some twenty-four years ago? Who cares now? For what reason?*

The answer came like a bolt of lightning—he saw it all in a flash! *It was to embarrass Judge McCowen and bring disgrace to his family! How could anyone be so low down as to pull a trick like this? If this is what newspaper people do, it's a dirty, disgusting business.* His mind recoiled at the thought of anyone doing this to a worthy man like Uncle Terrance. What a despicable act to do to another human being.

Burton sensed that Michael had seen something in the notebook that was alarming. His face was in shock. Burton asked, but Michael was unwilling to talk about the news he had just learned. This was now getting into his family, and although more than 24 years ago, it was still family business and should remain private.

Burton pressed. "Did you find anything interesting?"

"Not good, it's bad news," Michael muttered distractedly.

Burton pushed a little more, and finally, Michael reluctantly told him the facts that he had just learned. His Aunt Linda was a teenage mother, and the baby was sold or given to someone, somewhere. Now Linda was the judge's wife, living a very private life until Russell dug up the old history. He planned to threaten the judge with this knowledge. He would disclose it in his paper to the public. What an evil man, he would ruin the reputation of the judge and his wife.

"I can understand blackmailing the judge, but I don't get any connection to the murder of Russell. What was Coleman's motive to murder Russell? Was there some connection to the girl or the O'Dell family? No, nothing has developed that suggests a link," Burton replied.

They talked until very late that night and agreed to visit again soon. Michael went home very disturbed and did not sleep well that night. As a seasoned investigator, Burton reasoned that because it did not connect with Coleman directly, it was just another fact that got in the way in an investigation. *Set it aside for now. Go back to old-fashioned detective work—ask questions—get answers.*

The Gun from Dooley's Desk

. . .

The next day, Burton visited the Huntington Court clerk and asked to see the birth record of a child born in 1911 that a Mr. John Russell had enquired about. He examined the record, noted it was exactly as listed in the notebook. Nothing extra was there. He then drove to the hospital and asked about old birth records. The only record was in an old faded ledger. Dr. Nagle delivered a girl child on that date in 1911. The name was listed as the O'Dell child. No other information was available. It noted the baby was discharged from the hospital by Dr. Nagle.

Burton drove to the office of Dr. Nagle and introduced himself as an agent from the Pinkerton Detective Agency. The doctor had patients and could not see him. Burton asked the office nurse how he would find information about the delivery of a baby girl named O'Dell about twenty-four years ago. The nurse became agitated and asked Burton to return after four o'clock when the office would be closed. Burton returned and met the white-coated doctor in his office. The doctor introduced himself and his wife, Mrs. Nagle, the attractive auburn-haired lady in a crisp white nurse's uniform he had met earlier that day. She asked what information he wanted. Burton explained the notes from Russell's notebook and records he had seen at the clerk's office. They were the same. There was a baby born in 1911. They delivered it and took it out of the hospital.

"Where did it go?" he asked.

Dr. Nagle could not remember any specific baby by the name of O'Dell, and he denied any knowledge of Russell.

"I have practiced in Huntington for about 30 years. I have delivered several hundred babies during that time, and I cannot remember every baby. I'm sorry, I cannot help you." He stood and shook Burton's hand. "Goodbye, sorry we could not help you."

As Burton turned to leave, he noticed the framed diplomas on the wall—Dr. Nagle's from Indiana University School of Medicine, Mrs. Nagle's from St. Joseph School of Nursing. The name on her diploma was Phyllis O'Dell.

Burton stopped and turned back to face them. "The child's name was O'Dell. Your wife's maiden name was Phyllis O'Dell. That is more than a coincidence. Now I want some honest answers."

Dr. Nagle knew the detective was on to something, and he decided to tell some of the story to get him out of their lives for good.

"My wife is from a poor family in Erie Point. She attended high school in Huntington because the Erie Point School just went to the eighth grade. A local newspaper awarded her a full scholarship to nursing school. After graduating from nurse's training, she returned to Huntington and started as my office nurse when I opened my medical practice. Later, she earned her RN degree, and we have worked together all this time. Also, we have been married over thirty years."

The doctor continued. "Now the story of that baby. Phyllis has two nieces, Linda and Lydia O'Dell. Years ago,

The Gun from Dooley's Desk

when they were teenagers, these girls worked as hired girls for a family in Wabash. The older girl Linda got pregnant. She came to Huntington and stayed with us to avoid embarrassment to the family, and we delivered the child. That's the record you see at the clerk's office. That's about all the story."

"All except where you put the baby."

Phyllis stood in front of Burton and stared him straight in the eye. "The child was put with a wonderful family that legally adopted her, raised and educated her. We are not about to give any information that would ruin her life. As professionals, we are prohibited from divulging that information. Next time you contact us, you better have a court order, and our attorney will be present. Good-bye, Mr. Burton!"

Burton quickly left. He knew well enough when attacked by the head chicken in the flock, retreat. Don't mess with her. He was disappointed. None of the information he checked on added any value to the case. *No, something is missing, but what?*

On the way back to Wabash from Huntington, Burton decided to stop in Erie Point and see Mike O'Dell whom he had not met yet. Perhaps he could learn something about Linda O'Dell and the related events. He found Mike at the fire station, resting in an old wooden rocker with a large pillow cushion and smoking a Lucky Strike cigarette. The fire station cat was his only companion.

Burton introduced himself. "Do you know a Judge McCowen from Erie Point?"

Mike gave a hearty laugh. "Oh, hell yes I know him. He's my son-in-law, although I doubt if he brags about that very often. Him and my daughter have been married for years. Anymore they don't spend a lot of time with me. He's a real smart lawyer. I hear he's a good judge. He just got re-elected to a full term. I voted three times for him in the last election. I guess I shouldn't say that, but I damn well did." Mike chuckled at the thought of the free beer tokens at Dooley's. Burton and Mike talked awhile. Burton directed the conversation around to the present problem.

"Do you know of any reason the newspaper editor from Wabash would have any interest in a baby born over twenty years ago in Huntington to a teenage girl named Linda O'Dell? Would it be to embarrass the judge and his wife?"

Mike bristled. "You got it. Them God-damned Wabash Republicans are the devil. They will do anything to hurt us poor Democrats. My little Linda was a good girl. That rich bastard in Wabash got her pregnant. I read in the paper he died. I hope that piece of crap rots in hell forever. I say—good riddance of bad rubbish. He was a lousy son of a bitch."

Burton leaned next to Mike and spoke softly. "What's the name of that lousy son of a bitch from Wabash?"

Mike spat out the answer. "Coleman, Garl Coleman. Damn big shot. Well, he's rotting in hell now, and I ain't one bit sorry, no sir, not one little bit."

Burton heaved a sigh of relief. "I'm not sorry either. He deserved it. Thanks for talking to me, Mike. Don't rock that chair on the cat's tail or there will be hell to pay.

The Gun from Dooley's Desk

As he left, he slipped two Roi-Tan cigars in Mike's vest pocket.

Mike gave him a big smile. "Come back anytime, my friend. Maybe next time we can go down to Dooley's and visit awhile."

Burton smiled as he left. He now had one of the missing answers he needed to solve this case. It cost him only two five-cent cigars.

Chapter 12

SATURDAY MORNING WAS Jimmy's time to collect for the paper route. As he went from door to door, some residents had put his money in an envelope, leaving it in the space between the screen door and the front door. Some put it in the mailbox, and for others, he had to knock on the door to collect the 20 cents. It went smoothly on West Hill both sides, around Thorne Street, then he headed down the alley toward Roth Ave.

Several yards were being mowed with push mowers, and many sweating men wished the lawn work was done and they could take a break with a cool lemonade. Jimmy thought he was lucky to have a paper route and did not have to mow lawns in the summer. His ride was interrupted when he came to a person standing in the alley looking at the backyard of the Russell home. He recognized the man as Mr. Burton, the detective he brought to where he found the gun.

Jimmy rode up and boldly spoke to the man. "Hi there, Mr. Burton, remember me? I'm Jimmy Johnson. I showed you where I found the gun."

Burton smiled and replied, "Oh yes, I remember that day. You were a big help."

"What you are looking for now? Maybe I can help. I know every bit of this street by heart. I've delivered papers

The Gun from Dooley's Desk

here for a long time," Jimmy boasted. "I was here on my route the day Mr. Russell was shot. I heard the shot. I was here in the alley when those hobos walked by. I even saw them go in Mr. Coleman's garage."

Burton stiffened. "Say that again—you heard the shot and saw the hobos that day?"

"Yes! I saw them come out of Russell's backyard. They walked down to Coleman's garage and went in. I was here in the alley at that building right there." He pointed to an old shed next door.

Burton approached the bike and put his hand on the handlebar. "That's good to know. Did you tell anyone else about this bit of news?" he asked.

"No one ever asked me," Jimmy replied.

Burton knew he was on to something. "It would be a big favor to me if you showed me where they went in at Coleman's. I need to know exactly what you saw."

They walked down the alley to Coleman's garage, and Jimmy described exactly what he saw that afternoon. Burton took it all down in his notebook. Jimmy swelled with pride knowing his answers were written up in a detective's notebook—a real detective. As Burton was writing his notes, Jimmy unwittingly dropped the bombshell.

"A short time later, I was further down the alley when Mr. Coleman and that lady drove by me in the car."

That surprised Burton! He turned and looked at Jimmy directly. "What lady in Coleman's car?"

"The car passed by me real close. Mr. Coleman was driving. I had never seen that lady in the front seat before.

She looked right at me. She doesn't live around here. I know. I deliver papers every day, so I know all the ladies."

"What did this lady look like?" Burton asked.

"She had red hair. She was pretty for an older lady, about my mom's age," Jimmy replied.

"I really appreciate your help today, and I want to do you a favor. I have a book about the Pinkerton Agency that I am going to give you as a present. I'll have my office mail you a copy just for you." Burton drew close to Jimmy and smiled. "Oh, by the way, let's keep this chat just between us, OK? Remember, mum's the word."

Jimmy gave the Boy Scout sign and quickly agreed. "Yes sir, mum's the word. Scout's Honor."

Jimmy rode away to finish his route, and he was about to explode with pride. He had been a big help to a real Pinkerton detective, and he was going to get a real Pinkerton book coming in the mail—all his own. No other kid in town would have such a prize as that. Today, he was on top of the world. Maybe when he grew up, he would become a real Pinkerton detective. Would that be better than an airplane pilot? He would have to think about that.

Burton stood in the alley and pondered this fresh news. Now he suspected the other person was a woman, but what woman? *Could it be this Russell murder is going to be nothing but a messy "other scorned woman" seeking revenge case? How would Coleman fit into a scene like that? Damn it. No, it doesn't fit. This opens many new doors, too much for a warm day like this standing in a dusty alley.* Burton retired to his hotel room, set the electric fan in the open window and enjoyed a cold beer. He thought about the day's activities and

The Gun from Dooley's Desk

wondered if a visit with Michael would help. He placed a call.

"I'm off duty tomorrow. We can meet in the evening," Michael said.

As they settled into a cold Coke and sandwich at the Rock City Restaurant, the two men chatted about general man things. Eventually, he got to the subject of the other hobo.

"I have some interesting news for you. Remember that kid—Jimmy Johnson—you know, the kid that found the gun? Well, I happened to meet him in the alley behind Russell's house yesterday. We talked some, and he told me he was in the alley at the time of the shooting, saw the two hobos come out of Russell's backyard, walk down the alley and enter Coleman's garage. He was in a shed looking through some junk when it happened. He saw it all," Burton said. "I got his statement in writing."

Michael was surprised and pleased. "That's great news!"

"Yes! He saw Coleman's car up close as it left the alley. Coleman was driving. A woman was in the front seat, and he saw her real close as the car passed. Get this, a woman in Coleman's car, a few minutes after the shooting, and the kid saw her up close. The other hobo is a woman!" Burton added, smiling.

Michael digested this new fact. *A woman. Who would have such a need to kill the editor that she would be an accomplice?* "What woman? Not Mrs. Coleman or Mrs. Russell. Perhaps Russell was screwing around with some gal promising to marry her. She finds out he's not leaving home, or he's got her knocked up. So, she shoots him. A shot in the face is a shot of vengeance. He was an impressive guy. I can see some babe going gaga over him. I think you need to take a look at Russell's love life. The answer may be a scorned woman. We both know they can be deadly, especially some pissed off gal with a loaded gun!"

"Yes, I considered that," Burton replied, "but where does Coleman fit in? We know he was the shooter. The note said something in his past was discovered. That doesn't sound like a love triangle. No, I think it was something that they both shared. Both were afraid of Russell releasing some facts. I don't know what, but somehow that's the answer." Burton leaned back in his chair and reflected for a moment. "I have a feeling the woman is connected to Erie Point. That's where the gun came from, and maybe that's where she is from. You and I know the killer is Coleman. His suicide note says so, but that's gone. The only way this case is going to be solved is by finding that woman. She was there, and she was part of the murder. Find her, find the facts—the case is solved."

Michael agreed, "You're right! Find that woman! She's the answer to this case."

· · ·

The following Thursday, Jimmy finished the paper route and rushed home. He hurried into the house in time for his radio programs to start. He was in the living room next to the big Philco radio when his mother came in.

The Gun from Dooley's Desk

"The mailman brought you a package today. I put it on the dining room table for you. Be careful opening it."

Jimmy raced to the dining room and there on the table was a package from Indianapolis addressed to him, "Mr. Jimmy Johnson." Wow! His Pinkerton book had arrived. He ripped open the paper and saved the address sticker because it said "Pinkerton Detective Agency" on the label. Jimmy examined his new book—a story starting in the Old West with tales of train robberies, horse thieves, and bank robberies. There were several pictures of tough looking agents on horses holding Winchester rifles. They chased Jesse James, Butch Cassidy, and the Reno Gang. There were automobile thieves, murders, and all kinds of crime right up to now. Jimmy was excited. "What a great book, and it's mine!"

His mother looked in and inspected the book. "You know, it would be nice if we could get that Detective Burton to sign this book for you. I'll bet he would if we ask him." That evening, she called the hotel and asked Burton if he would do that.

"Yes, I'll be happy to come out and sign his book. In fact, I have a favor to ask you. I need Jimmy to look at a person. Maybe he could help identify someone," Burton said.

"I'm sure he will be delighted to help," Jimmy's mother replied.

The next day after signing the book, Burton and Jimmy drove to Huntington. The first stop was the florist shop where Burton purchased a nice flower arrangement. Then he drove to Dr. Nagle's office. Burton parked a few doors down away from the front door. He instructed

Jimmy to take the flowers into the office and ask for Mrs. Nagle.

When she appeared to receive the flowers, Jimmy looked carefully at her. He told her the flowers were an apology from Mr. Burton and that he was sorry about their last meeting. Phyllis took the flowers with a big smile and thanked Jimmy for making the delivery. She opened her purse and gave him a dime tip. Jimmy returned to the car where Burton was anxiously waiting.

"Yep, that's her. That's the woman I saw in Coleman's car that day. I would know her anyplace," he stated positively.

Burton almost shouted with joy. Another answer to the puzzle was solved! He got it with a publicity book and a bouquet of flowers.

The following day, Burton called Mrs. Nagle. She was in a better mood now after receiving the flowers. He asked if he could talk to her alone, discuss the options and reach some agreement.

"Come to the office tonight about 7:30. I will meet you there. The staff will be gone, and the doctor will be at the hospital until about nine o'clock. We can talk privately," she replied.

Burton arrived at 7:30 p.m. as instructed. Phyllis greeted him in a friendly manner and offered him a seat.

"Would you care for sherry or perhaps a whiskey?" she asked. She wore pearls and a pretty blue dress, modest and fashionable, which complemented her blue eyes.

Burton politely declined a drink, and Phyllis poured herself a sherry then sat across the table from him. Burton proceeded to tell her he could prove she was the other

The Gun from Dooley's Desk

person with Coleman. He had a witness, a new witness that only he knew about. Burton also told her he now knew Coleman's motive for the killing. Coleman fathered the child with the teenager Linda. Burton continued, saying he knew her reason to be a part of the killing was to protect her husband and agreed Russell was a blackmailer and needed to be shot. He offered her a deal.

"If you confess, I will explain my investigation shows it was because Coleman threatened you and you were afraid. You accompanied him out of fear for your life. As part of the deal, you must disclose the name and address of the child." He leaned back in his chair. "OK?" he asked hopefully.

"You can go to hell. Think about this! Russell, Coleman, and Parker are dead, all because of that girl. My husband and I are the only people who know, and we are not telling you or anyone else. You stop this now, or I will claim you attempted to assault me sexually, but I fought back." She had the phone in her hand, ready to call the police. "Now get out and don't come back, Mr. Burton," she ordered.

Burton left quickly. *Damn! That redhead is a tough cookie—don't mess with her!*

On the drive back to Wabash, Burton reflected on his progress. *Without the Coleman note and without a confession from Phyllis, there is no case. Nothing can be proven. There are several leads but few solid, usable facts.* Back in his hotel room, he thoughtfully completed his weekly progress report to the office. Burton listed the interviews he had conducted, the sites he had personally examined and the records he had reviewed. He wrote his summary. "This case has some difficult issues. Our order is to find the real killer of Russell. That killer is Garl Coleman but not provable; the note is destroyed. Coleman's motive to commit the murder is known. The second hobo has been identified, but the witness is a twelve-year-old kid. The gun has been identified as stolen from Dooley's by persons unknown. Who? There are no fingerprints, no tangible evidence, and few solid provable facts."

From his years of experience, Burton knew that cases have a curve from start to finish. The beginning examination produces evidence, and that discloses new evidence, leading to the principals in the case. Once the facts and the principals are linked, the case is solved. That was not happening here. He completed his report. "Unless there is a significant change in the case, I believe it is not worth further time and energy to continue. Allen Burton, Agent."

The supervisor in Indianapolis read the report with apprehension. The customer was a big rich movie studio. They did not complain about the daily costs and charges. He did not want to disappoint them. He mailed Burton his orders. "Give it one more try. This is an important client."

The Gun from Dooley's Desk

Chapter 13

SEVERAL TIMES EACH YEAR, the Erie Point families gathered for a big picnic. This gave everyone a chance to catch up on the family news. There was always plenty of food, toys for the kids and cold beer for the men. This year, it was held again at Hanging Rock, a natural rock formation hanging over the Salamonie River close to the junction of the Wabash River. It was an old Indian camping ground and a favorite picnic grounds for the locals who knew its location just outside of Erie Point.

This weekend, the judge and Linda could not be there. Terrance had a blister on his foot and had trouble walking. But a large family group gathered with much fried chicken and all the trimmings. Kids ran and played, and the women visited and caught up on the latest news. Lydia had a new Maytag wringer washer, the envy of all the ladies. The men smoked, played cards and enjoyed a cold beer out of the ice sack. Dr. Nagle told about moving to a new location near the hospital, leaving the house where he started practice. John McCaffery was putting down a driven well at the funeral home—a deep well.

Michael had just put a set of Montgomery Ward's Riverside tires on the state police car. "The Ford V-8 handles great, and I hope the tires will be good in the snow too," he said with pride.

The Gun from Dooley's Desk

Later, the men made ice cream and took turns cranking the machine. When it was done, the treat was ice cream and strawberry short cake. They all sat around enjoying the dessert. Phyllis and Michael sat at a table together. She asked about his state police job and his new lady friend.

"When are we going to get to meet her? You should bring her to a family picnic sometime soon." The talk turned to local items, and she asked if there was anything new in the Russell case. It seemed someone had hired a detective named Burton. Michael told her he had met Burton.

"I understand a well-to-do person is seeking information about the Russell murder and willing to pay big bucks to get answers," Michael confided.

"I hear Russell was a powerful man, and he scared a lot of people. But he was not so powerful when he was lying in the petunia patch," Phyllis remarked.

Michael sensed something in that statement and paused before replying. "I never knew the man, but you are right. Getting shot in a flower bed is not a great way to go." *How the hell did she know he was killed in the petunias?* Michael thought.

Later, after the picnic was over, Michael stopped at home in Erie Point to visit with his mom and dad. John took the flashlight and went out to check the well-driving equipment in the side lot pumping out the new well. While he was gone, Michael spoke to his mother.

"Mom, I need to have a very private word with you. Please help me."

"Sure son, what do you need? Money, advice, someone to iron your shirts and darn your socks? That's what moms are for. You are eating all that fried restaurant food. You need more vegetables, I can tell. You look peaked," Lydia replied.

"No Mom, it's not that at all. This is serious—I have troubles."

Lydia came to the table and sat down. "What kind of troubles?" she asked.

"I've been meeting with Allen Burton, the Pinkerton guy. He's working on the Russell case and the Coleman death. A lot is going on you need to know about. First, Coleman committed suicide. He left a note and can you believe he confessed shooting Russell? But the note is gone—destroyed—nothing can be proven now. The strange thing is that somehow Doctor Nagle and Aunt Phyllis are involved in the case. They delivered a baby born to Aunt Linda when she was a teenager. We think Russell planned to use it against the judge for political reasons.

"The gun came from Dooley's. Someone in Erie Point supplied it to Coleman; he didn't own a gun. Lastly, Aunt Phyllis and I were talking at the picnic. She made a strange statement that worried me. She said, 'Russell was a powerful man. He scared a lot of people, but he was not so powerful when he was lying in the petunia patch.'" Michael took a deep breath. "How did she know the murder scene was in a petunia patch?"

Lydia was shaken by what she just heard. She took a few seconds to clear her thoughts. "I need to tell you this before John gets back," she said quietly, glancing at the

The Gun from Dooley's Desk

door. "You are right on some things. But there is a lot more to the Russell story than you know. Russell was a man determined to destroy many people and ruin their lives. Not only the judge and Linda but also Dr. Nagle and Phyllis. They would lose their medical licenses, perhaps even stand trial. Coleman and his family would suffer lasting embarrassment even affecting their lives and their business.

The baby girl is now a responsible adult. Her life would be devastated. Russell was an evil man—he had to be stopped—and sometimes drastic steps are necessary. It had to happen. Coleman had a reason. He was determined to do it, and he threatened Phyllis to get her to help him. Now be strong when I tell you this. I took the gun from Dooley's desk."

With that announcement, Lydia was visibility shaken, but Michael was in shock!

"My God, what are you saying? You just confessed to being an accessory to murder. I am a law officer. I must report any crimes I encounter. I'm not going to arrest my mother. I'm going to pretend I did not hear that from you." His mind recorded the facts. *My Mom and Dooley's gun. Oh, hell yes! That answers a lot of questions.*

He corralled his thoughts. *That baby dominates this case; somehow, she keeps popping up every time something new is added.* "Do you know where the baby girl went, and where is she now?" he asked his mom directly.

Lydia shook her head. "No, Dr. Nagle and Phyllis placed the child in a good Christian home. They have never told anyone. Phyllis told us several years ago the girl was starting college. Her life has been good so far.

Identifying her now would be a disaster. It's not going to happen. Not from us." She glanced at the door again. "Hush up now; John is coming back. He doesn't know about any of this."

"Are you telling me you two women cooked all this up by yourselves?" Michael exclaimed, astounded at what he was hearing.

"Yes," answered Lydia. "Be quiet now. John's coming back."

. . .

The local churches in Wabash helped out those families that were on the dole from County Relief Services. The Presbyterian church had a group led by Reverend Warner that gave additional food to poor families. Lucille Coleman and her mother both contributed to this worthwhile ministry. The Parker family was on relief now that they had no wage earner in the house. Reverend Warner met the family when he did the funeral service for Billy Parker and felt sorry for them. His group took a box of food to their house. They appreciated the gift, and the pastor asked for their Bible. He said he would like to pray for the family. Mrs. Parker went to Billy's room and retrieved the family Bible.

When Reverend Warner opened the old, large leather-bound Bible, he discovered a sealed envelope marked "OFFICIAL POLICE BUSINESS." After prayers, they discussed what to do with the envelope, which looked very official. Lucille suggested giving it to her friend who was a state policeman. He would see that it got

The Gun from Dooley's Desk

to the proper place. She called Michael to stop by her house and pick it up.

That evening, Michael picked up the envelope and took it home. He was not sure what to do. He was reluctant to open it, but he did. Michael carefully removed the contents, a single page of paper. The letterhead stated, "Coleman Cabinet & Fine Furniture Factory" with a half page handwritten letter. He stared in utter disbelief! *My God, this is the Coleman suicide note!* His mind was in turmoil. *How did this turn up now? Parker told Burton that he burned it, but here it is in the real. This changes everything!*

That evening, Michael sat at his kitchen table with the confession before him, studying what to do. When they thought the note was destroyed, the case was over, but now it opened dangerous doors. *I must be careful, I want to obey the law, yet I must protect my mother and Aunt Phyllis. Nobody knows I have this note. Somehow, I must use it wisely to protect the family and perhaps my job.*

Michael called the commanding officer of his post, got permission to take the note to the new crime laboratory, have it photographed and have several certified copies made. When the lab called to report the item copied successfully, he drove there and picked up the copies. The crime lab always kept one copy of everything they made on file.

He phoned Burton and arranged a meeting on his day off. They met at Hal's Highway Grill, selected a corner table and greeted each other warmly. Burton was down. He told Michael about the progress report to the office.

"Not good," he said dismally. "They told me to give it one more try. Without the note or a confession, there is no hope to finish this case. This will not look good on my record with the company. If you don't produce results, you are not promoted."

Michael suggested a solution. "What if you had a certified copy of the note? What could be worked out if you had that as a fact? Who else would you need to complete the case? You could prove Coleman was the shooter with the note. There is nothing to tie the Nagles to the murder; they delivered a child twenty-four years ago. The history of the gun is incomplete. How could all this be sidetracked?"

Burton stared at Michael with a puzzled look and paused for a moment, digesting what Michael just told him. "There are some new developments you are not aware of yet. I'm not sure I should confide in you, but I will. First, I have a positive identification of Phyllis Nagle with Coleman in the car a few minutes after the shooting. The problem is, the witness is a twelve-year-old kid. Courts don't take favorably to twelve-year-old witnesses.

The second important fact. I have a witness, the girl's father, who positively identified Garl Coleman as the man who molested the O'Dell girl and got her pregnant at 15 years old. That is the motive for the killing. Russell learned about the child's pregnancy. Coleman knew he got her pregnant and that would make him a child molester. Coleman had to kill Russell to cover it all up. We don't know the motive of the second shooter, how the gun got to Coleman, or if the child fits into this at all—yet it seems to be tied together. How could the note appear now? Parker burned it to cover his ass. He told me so himself."

The Gun from Dooley's Desk

Michael smiled. "Parker was a damned liar. I have a certified copy of the original Coleman suicide note in my possession. Trust me, I do. It's a certified copy from the state police crime lab. How can we make this work for you, yet protect my family interests and still be within the law?"

"I see where you are heading, and I want to work with you. Without the note, there is no case. However, I see your need to protect the family. Much of the evidence about them cannot be proven anyway," Burton replied. "Perhaps we could agree if I worded my final report carefully." He took a moment to gather his thoughts.

"John Russell was murdered because he discovered a secret in the past of a fifteen-year-old girl who delivered a baby out of wedlock. Twenty-four years later, that girl is now the wife of a prominent elected official. Russell was prepared to blackmail that elected official to embarrass the family and discourage further political activity. Coleman learned of this, realized he had impregnated the girl, and if this material were released, he would be found out—exposed as a child molester. Coleman murders Russell before this material is released. Later, Coleman is consumed with guilt and commits suicide by carbon monoxide poisoning. In the certified copy of Coleman's suicide note, Coleman confesses to the murder and explains the motive, to protect him and his family from public disgrace.

"Coleman had an accomplice that supplied the gun, stolen from Dooley's sometime in the past. After a lengthy search, a suspect was identified and interrogated, but positive identification, acceptable to a court, was not achieved. The gun is a problem. The gun was stolen. When and by whom is not provable. There are no fingerprints on the gun.

"After an extensive investigation, I feel no further evidence would add additional information to this case. We offer this conclusion based on the discovered facts: the arrest, conviction, and death of Jerry Lester had no connection with the Russell murder." Burton took a sip of his coffee, which was getting cold. "Will that satisfy you? That is factual, describes the case in a true manner, and yet keeps your family at a distance. I do not know if the court is going to do anything about this case, but right now I don't see any action."

Michael paused. "As I see it, the Russell murder is solved by Coleman's confession. There are no other persons that can be positively identified, no trail of the gun from Dooley's to Coleman, no other persons that could be connected or charged with a crime. OK, that's acceptable to me."

"Would you like to read my report when I finish before I mail it in?" Burton asked.

"No, we agreed to the content, and I trust you to write it up that way," Michael replied.

"I'll make you a copy and mail it to your house, a copy just for you," Burton said.

They shook hands and parted.

For Burton, this was over. For Michael, he was still unsure about the future. Burton was preparing to leave Wabash for the second time and was sure he would never return, at least not on this case. Investigations have a way of driving themselves in one direction or another. This case uncovered secrets twenty-four years old that drove the case in many directions. As he was packing and preparing to check-out, he reflected on the case. *Who are these people?*

The main actor in the play was John Russell, a man who concealed his evil actions behind a façade of respectability that was the cause of bad actions by others. Coleman was also an evil person, masquerading as a solid citizen, now dead although he probably deserved it. He thought about Billy Parker, a man in over his head, doomed to failure. He followed a chief that lacked moral character. *Billy's dead now; it was a stupid thing to do, but he is still dead. Chief Moore, struck down by the stress of this case, felt a need to create evidence to convict Lester. But why? Poor Lester was already sentenced, banished to a life of poverty and stupidity, a nobody. However, his life took on an expanded role that stretched from Wabash to Hollywood.* As he backed the car out of the parking lot, he wondered what the future would bring to those people whose lives had been touched by the case.

Burton arrived at the Cass Street intersection and turned south on the highway toward Indianapolis. He drove across the river bridge and climbed the hill south of town. At the top, he looked back. He viewed the beautiful river valley, the neat city of Wabash so calm and serene, probably a nice place to live. But he had scratched under the surface, uncovered dark secrets from the past that were unpleasant and proved deadly. Burton waved and exclaimed to himself, "Goodbye Wabash, may our paths never cross again!"

Chapter 14

KATHY RODE HER BICYCLE to work that day; it was only about a half mile from home. She was a college student working for the new Indiana State Police Crime Laboratory located at New Haven, just outside Fort Wayne. She worked two days a week, filing reports and helping with general office duties. Today, she filed the tracking reports for the open cases, the folders that had been used but not returned to the proper cabinets. It was not a busy day. She completed the file work and then worked on the odd stuff in the basket. She found a place for all the unlisted reports, except one.

"What do I do with this?" she asked her chief. She held up a photocopy from the basket.

"What is that?" he asked.

"It is something Trooper McCaffery brought in to have copied. It's not part of any investigation, so there is no case number on it. It's just something he wanted copied. This is our copy. Do I save it or throw it away?" Kathy replied.

"Let me see it; it's probably a throwaway."

He carefully read the note, realized it was a suicide note, and evidently it was a confession to a murder—signed by a Garl Coleman! This note definitely required

The Gun from Dooley's Desk

some additional investigation. "I will take care of this one," he replied.

The lab chief called Major Hoffman, the commander of the Peru State Police Post, and suggested a meeting with Major Hoffman and Trooper McCaffery as soon as possible. The lab chief explained it just involved some paperwork that needed to be cleared up. The meeting was set for the following Thursday at the laboratory, and Trooper McCaffery was instructed to be there.

When Michael arrived at the meeting and saw Major Hoffman, his senior officer, he was very concerned. He thought it was just some paperwork problem; now he knew it was more. The major had reviewed Michael's work reports and was very pleased with what he found. Michael was very careful with the written reports, very complete, and very thorough. The major wished all his staff was so diligent. Some staff members were careless filing written reports. They met in the staff workroom, all three seated at the table. Michael was uncomfortable with two high ranking officers flanking him. The lab chief opened a folder containing only the Coleman letter photocopy, slid it across the table to the major and turned to Michael.

"Please explain this to us. If it is real, this is serious business."

Michael realized now was the time to be strong. "I cannot tell you if it is real or fake. It was given to me by a Reverend Warner of Wabash. He found it hidden in a Bible when he was giving a prayer service at the private home of a deceased Wabash policeman. This note was in possession of the Wabash Police Chief, Bill Parker, who apparently had found it. A Pinkerton Agent named Allen Burton was in Wabash working on several cases, and Parker shared the note with him. Burton told me he held the note in his hands and read it. The note was misplaced when Parker suddenly died, was later found by the Reverend Warner, who for some reason gave it to me.

"I had certified copies made because I did not know if it was real or not. But I wanted to have a copy in a safe place at the crime lab if it were ever needed as evidence. I never met Mr. Coleman although I know the other family members quite well. I expect to become engaged to Lucille Coleman, the daughter, in the near future. I did not know Mr. Russell. I was not in Wabash at the time of the murder or the trial." Michael paused. "I did not know what to report to my senior officer. There is no criminal investigation involving Coleman. The Russell murder trial is completed, a defendant found guilty, and the convicted party is dead. That case is closed."

Major Hoffman, being the senior officer in the room, took charge. "Thank you, Officer McCaffery, for your explanation. We will conduct an internal investigation. You are not suspected of any wrongdoing. We need to confirm the facts are as you presented them today. I'm quite sure they are, but we cannot let anything slip by that could embarrass the department. I know you realize that. In the meantime, continue to perform your duties as you have been, we are proud of you."

As Michael drove the peppy 1935 Ford V-8 back to Wabash, he breathed a sigh of relief. *I came out OK. I wonder, what's coming next?*

The Gun from Dooley's Desk

• • •

Trooper McCaffery was on road patrol west of Huntington on US 24 in the afternoon. He observed a flatbed truck traveling west with a load of old wire fence. It looked as if it had backed into something and broken off the left tail light. The trooper turned on the patrol car's flashing red light to pull the truck over. He walked to the driver's side to ask for the license and registration. The driver jumped out in a panic, took a wild swing at Michael but missed, jumped over the side ditch and ran into the woods. Michael took out his gun, ordered the other man out of the truck and asked for some identification. The man produced a Miami County "Relief" card with his name on it. He claimed they were working for a nearby farmer cleaning out some old wire fence, and they were hauling it to the dump.

"Who is that driver and what's his problem? It has to be more than a broken tail light. Is he wanted for something?"

At first, the man was hesitant to say anything. Under threat of going to jail, he soon agreed to tell what he knew.

"The driver's name is Lenny. I don't know the last name. Lenny claims he is the best friend of Jerry Lester, the man convicted of murder in Wabash. Lenny bragged he was with Jerry Lester in Wabash on the day of the murder. He is afraid the police are looking for him as an accomplice to the murder. Lenny knows the second hobo has not been arrested. He believes the police got his name from Lester in his confession and are now looking to arrest him. He's afraid. That's why he resisted arrest and ran."

Trooper McCaffery ordered the man to turn the truck around and drive it back to the farm where they started. The radio in the police car was not working properly. He could not reach headquarters. This required him to drive back to the Huntington Police Department to use their telephone. McCaffery reported the event that took place to his dispatcher at the Peru Post. The dispatcher asked him to standby, they would call back in a few minutes. When the desk officer called, Trooper McCaffery was informed that there was no warrant for a man named Lenny or for any unknown second man claiming a connection with Lester in Wabash. If the driver did not actually strike the trooper, then let him go. He was suffering under some delusion about his importance in the Wabash murder case or may be intoxicated. You are instructed to write a detailed description of the man for future reference."

A week later, a body was found by a farmer about a mile south of US 24 in a swampy area. There was no identification on the body, but he was recognized by a tattoo on his upper arm of a circus trapeze lady. His name was Lenny Nickels, a former circus worker. His father was a close relative to the Lester family in Peru, Indiana. Lenny and Jerry Lester attended grade school together as youths and parted ways in high school. Later, each man worked for the Cole Brothers Circus for many years, traveling the country together.

The Gun from Dooley's Desk

WABASH
ELKS LODGE
BULLETIN

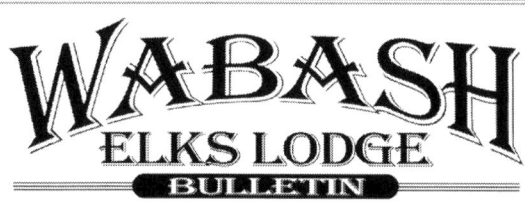

This month, our Lodge voted three new members into our Fraternal organization. Be sure to meet and greet them and make them welcome in our Lodge home. We are all brothers in the Lodge, all Americans, all eager to help our fellow man.

The new members and their sponsors are:

Honorable Judge Terrance McCowen
Wabash Circuit Court, Erie Point.
His sponsor is Frank Plum.

Richard "Bill" String,
Owner String Fine Furniture Store, Market Street, Wabash.
His sponsor is Joe Speer.

Michael McCaffery,
Indiana State Trooper, Wabash & Erie Point.
His sponsor is Oliver Pezzell.

This Saturday night is the monthly dinner dance
(Larry Lewis Band) at the Lodge.
Come out for the evening to dine and dance and
meet these new members.
The prime rib dinner is prepared by our Chef Randy, his specialty.
Enjoy a delicious meal and a great band for only $2.00 per person.

Support your Elks Lodge brothers and the good work
they do in the community.

Allen Hill, Secretary

The Gun from Dooley's Desk

Chapter 15

POLICE CHIEF MOORE had been on medical leave for over a year recuperating from the massive heart attack he had suffered. He followed the doctor's orders, taking his medicines and getting plenty of rest, with little improvement. He did not feel any better or get stronger. He was so debilitated, he needed help walking or going up steps. He was too weak to drive the car. This was depressing to the former football star and athletic hero. His wife Fern was concerned about his future. He was extremely depressed even suicidal. She hid his service revolver from him.

The Moores had been members of the Falls Avenue Church for twenty years. They lived just a short distance away and could walk to the church. That summer, the church held a big event. A huge white tent was erected on the empty lot next to the church. A large sign proclaimed, "THE BILLY SUNDAY TENT REVIVAL." The revival lasted a week. Each night, a different preacher would conduct the service, Billy Sunday himself preaching on Friday night and Sunday morning. Homer Rodeheaver would be there in person on Sunday. He would sing, play his famous trombone, and direct the music. Sunday and Rodeheaver appearing the same week was a significant event for this popular church and a big event for Wabash as well.

The church had many members besides the Moore family. Court clerk Bob Miller was a deacon in the church and was very active in the church's ministries. The revival was well attended each night. The singing filled the tent. The inspirational sermons were uplifting to people stuck in the depression with little hope. Wednesday night, a woman preacher was the program—many attended to hear a woman preach. This was not a common occurrence. Her message was on "Health and Sickness." Her sermon was compelling, and the audience reacted to her powerful words.

At the climax of her presentation, she called out for anyone needing help to speak up now. She faced the crowd and commanded, "Repent now! Come clean with God." From his wheelchair in the front row, Zeno slowly rose and struggled to make his way forward. Several men helped him climb the three steps to the stage and provided a chair for him.

The preacher stood behind Zeno, raised her Bible over his head and announced, "Here is a sick man. He will not get better until he cleanses his mind and spirit, confesses his sins, and repents! Then—and only then—will his body receive the helpful cure that only God can give. Doctors have not helped—medicine is powerless!"

She turned to Zeno and pronounced, "You know in your heart the pain your sins are causing. Get rid of them now! Repent now—come clean with God!" Then she paused.

Zeno was overcome with emotion. With great effort, he stood and held on to the chair for support. He faltered, then took a breath and shouted, "Yes! I have sinned. I need to confess my sins. I want to come clean with God. I beat that man Lester to confess, and I beat him so bad, I put him in the hospital. I wrote the confession—it was all a lie. I lied in court. My testimony was a lie. I am so sorry. Please God, forgive me of my sins. I repent now. Please God, help me get well!"

He sank down in the chair, utterly exhausted, a weight lifted from his weakened body. Perspiration covered his face as he cried out, "Thank God. I feel better already."

The revival audience was shocked and in awe. They had just witnessed a once in a lifetime experience. They stood, cheered, and applauded this emotional event.

One man shouted, "A miracle has just occurred tonight—right here on Falls Avenue!"

The preacher broke into a song, the congregation eagerly joining in. The piano rang out the hymn, "TELL IT TO JESUS," and the audience enthusiastically sang the part: "Do you have sins that to men's eyes are hidden? Tell it to Jesus alone." Tears streamed down Fern's face. The minister offered a prayer for Zeno. The audience stood and added their voices.

Deacon Bob Miller observed Zeno and the preacher. He was pleased Zeno had a miracle work for him that night, but he had deep concerns about the confession. *It was all a lie!* He could not understand what he just heard. His mind recalled the chief of police in the witness box, putting his hand on the Bible and being sworn in by the clerk. Then he gave his sworn testimony. *Now he says it's all a lie? How can this be? What happens now, is he charged with perjury?* The questions remained unanswered. These were uncharted waters. He retired to the darkened church, knelt in prayer and asked God's guidance on the trouble he knew was coming.

The next morning, clerk Miller reported to the judge on what had occurred at the church. "The testimony of Chief Moore was false. The Lester confession was a lie. The chief wrote it. Parker participated, and it was all a lie to convict Lester. Now Lester is dead. That was his confession at the church, freely given before a tent full of people."

Judge McCowen was appalled. He remembered the chief on the witness stand giving his damaging testimony, the confession that convicted Lester. His mind had one big question. *How could a solid church member, a sworn law officer, and a Christian do this?*

The judge then mulled over the next question. *What do I do now?* He poured a fresh cup of black coffee, picked up the phone and called Prosecutor Frank Plum for a meeting in the judge's chambers. "Please, make it quick!" he commanded.

• • •

Judge McCowen, court clerk Bob Miller, and Prosecutor Frank Plum were seated at the table in the judge's chambers. The office clerk was instructed they were not to be disturbed. Bob Miller carefully related the events he witnessed the previous night at the church and specifically Chief Moore's confession. He told of the large crowd of church people who heard the chief's public confession of perjury in the Lester trial.

"It is going to be common knowledge on the street soon. What do we do about it now?"

Frank was alarmed. "This entire case was about that confession. We trusted the chief. There was no reason to doubt the confession was legally obtained and freely given. The chief testified to that, and Officer Parker substantiated that on the stand under oath. If the confession is removed, there is no real case. All the other evidence was supportive of the confession but weak on its own merits. My God! Do we arrest Zeno for perjury? He is a sick man, half dead. This would kill him for sure. I trusted him completely. I never thought to confirm the stuff he gave me. When the paper gets this, we will look like a bunch of fools. Damn, if you can't trust a man like Zeno, who in the hell can you trust?" Frank exclaimed.

Judge McCowen cleared his throat. "I have not looked up the rules for a retrial in a case like this, but there are some simple laws. A retrial is granted when there is proven malfeasance on the part of a court officer, that would include Zeno. However, the accused is now dead, so any retrial would bring no relief to the defendant. His relatives might want to clear his name, but the county is paying for a retrial and would not want one unless ordered to do so."

"I suggest we agree on some course of action, some position we can unite on. We must stand together on this—we are not the problem, Zeno is the problem. I feel we must have an answer ready and be united when the questions come," Bob Miller added.

The Gun from Dooley's Desk

"Zeno caused this problem. He must carry the blame for the results. Let's lay all the blame on Zeno and Parker. They lied about the confession. They perjured their testimony—they are to blame. We had no idea this was false testimony," Frank agreed.

"It's easy to lay the blame on Zeno, who's a real sick man, and Parker who is dead. I agree they are to blame and we must say so. But we all share the burden of not examining the evidence in more detail. When Lester recanted his confession, I just thought it was the attempt of a guilty man to escape his judgment. I should have been open to studying his claims. As a final thought, if a retrial occurs, we must be just as eager to find a man innocent as we were to find him guilty. I agree we must stick together. This could be difficult. Much depends on what a guy in California named Les Lang decides to do when he hears the news. There might be a Pinkerton guy back in town asking questions again, and that's not good," Judge McCowen remarked.

Bob Miller looked at his watch and stood up. "I agree with you; those two are to blame. We must say so when questioned. I will prepare a release to give to the press when they show up here, and I will give you each a copy. Right now, I've work to do."

• • •

Ruth Clary and her husband had been members of the Falls Avenue Church as long as they lived in Wabash. They met their first friends there, and they were close with the Moore family especially Fern Moore. Fern volunteered at the church, and Ruth often helped her. That ended when Ruth went to work full time at the local newspaper. It was an excellent job in the depression. Jobs were few, particularly for women. Ruth worked extra hard; she wanted to keep her job. She loved what she did, and the family needed the money she earned working. Ruth was not a reporter, but she often gave bits of information to the reporters to follow up on. One time she reported a sidewalk that could be dangerous—they kidded her—the news had to be more stimulating than a broken sidewalk.

Ruth and her husband attended the evening services of the Revival. She took notes on attendance, sermon details, and other items of interest, which she provided to the paper's social editor. The newspaper included a short write up of the Revival every day. Having a Billy Sunday Revival in Wabash for a week was a well-attended and newsworthy event. They were impressed with the Wednesday night sermon. It offered a path for sick people to find a cure. The woman pastor presented a powerful, emotional message and delivered it in a sincere manner. Ruth and her husband had never heard a woman pastor before.

They were astounded when their friend Zeno Moore took the stage to repent and confessed in order to regain his health. They were happy their friend publicly recanted his sins. Perhaps he would get better soon. They gave Fern their best wishes and participated in the group prayer for Zeno. After the service, they visited with other members. All agreed it was a great service. The subject of Zeno never came up.

The Gun from Dooley's Desk

By the time she got home, she had a disturbing thought in her mind. *Zeno announced to all present that the testimony he gave in a murder trial was false; this was not just a moral sin—this was perjury.* The couple discussed the problem together. They were bothered by the fact that this was a severe crime. They prayed about the problem and felt better, but still, no answer came. Ruth decided to talk to the reporter that covered court news the next day.

Early the next morning, Ruth stopped at the desk of the reporter, but he had not come in yet. She left a note to come by her desk as she had some information for him. Not a broken sidewalk this time.

When the reporter arrived, he stopped at her desk. Before she could say anything, he volunteered, "You can't guess what I just learned. Last night at a local church, Chief Moore confessed in public that he committed perjury in the Lester murder trial! Can you believe that? The chief of police admitting perjury in public?"

"Yes, I believe it, I was there! I heard it and here are notes I took," Ruth responded.

"Before you say a word, let's go to see the editor. This is something special. We need some guidance on this," the reporter said.

The two walked to the editor's office, knocked and were invited in. Editor Perry asked, "What can I do for you two so early in the morning?"

"I attended the Revival last night. I took notes for the paper, and I heard Zeno Moore publicly admit that he committed perjury at the Lester trial," Ruth replied.

"I had breakfast at Mike's Grill this morning, and I heard about it there. It's news! A hundred people were there last night, and they all heard it. How do you want me to handle it? What can we print?" the reporter added.

Perry was alarmed about the news he just learned. "Here is Mrs. Russell coming in. Let's run this by her. She has some definite ideas about these things."

He went to the office door and spoke to Mrs. Russell in the hall. She came into the editor's office and greeted Ruth and the reporter. Perry elaborated on the situation to her.

Mrs. Russell walked to the window and looked outside for a moment. Then she turned to face the others. "Last night, a friend called me with the news about Chief Moore. We must remember the story is not about Mr. Russell or Chief Moore. The story is about Jerry Lester. We must stick to facts. The ramblings of a gravely sick man in a very emotional setting are not facts no matter how many people heard him. Right now, it's just gossip.

"If a warrant is ever issued by the prosecutor's office for Chief Moore, that's a story. If the court orders a retrial in the Lester case, that's our story. Perry can call on the judge and see if he has any statement, but I doubt the court will have any reply ready yet. In answer to your question, just run a report in the social column about the Revival last night and omit any reference to Chief Moore. Another thing—if a Mr. Burton, a Pinkerton agent, comes here again, send him directly to me," she stated.

The article appeared in The Wabash Daily News, local church news column.

The Gun from Dooley's Desk

The Falls Avenue Church Tent Revival has been well attended all week. The evening sermon starts at seven o'clock. Wednesday night's sermon on Health and Sickness was delivered to a full house. The powerful message resulted in a public confession by a member, much to the amazement of the audience.

Sunday morning will be the major event. World famous Evangelist Billy Sunday will preach. Homer Rodeheaver will sing his famous gospel songs and play his trombone. This is the first appearance for Sunday and Rodeheaver in the Wabash area; they are usually booked into larger cities. The Falls Avenue Church is very pleased with the response to the Revival Week Program.

. . .

When Mr. Ellis returned from the Army, he and his wife built their new home on Riverside Road in Peru. They were part of the group that started the Riverside Church. They worked, and it grew. They watched the new church building being constructed near their home in 1929. Both devoted much energy to the church and enjoyed every minute of their services. The depression was hard on churches, many folded, many just got by—a few flourished. Riverside was one that retained most of its members, kept a paid minister and a part-time music director. But those luxuries didn't come easily. It took constant effort to keep everything moving along.

That is why Mr. and Mrs. Ellis drove to Wabash to observe the attendance at the Billy Sunday Revival. Their church was considering having a major revival the following year. A church had to guarantee a considerable amount of money to attract an Evangelist like Billy Sunday. That required a sizable attendance and a good response when the giving basket was passed—not an easy thing in the heartland during the depression.

They attended the Wednesday night sermon for a special reason. They saw and heard a female preacher for the first time. Mrs. Ellis thought she was terrific—women know a great deal about health and treating sickness. Mr. Ellis was not sure God intended women to be preachers, but he admitted the sermon was powerful. They were both impressed when a man got up and confessed his sins to get a cure. This was no ordinary man. They heard it was the chief of police. He confessed to lying at a trial and beating a man to confess a crime he didn't do. This was a shocking event.

"God help that poor man. He has many sins," Mrs. Ellis remarked.

The next morning, Mrs. Ellis and her neighbor sat on her front porch enjoying a cup of coffee as Mr. Ellis mowed the front lawn. He liked to mow before it got too hot. Mrs. Ellis was telling her neighbor about the extraordinary event they saw the previous evening at the Wabash Church Revival.

"It was a powerful sermon delivered by a woman. A sinner confessed, and the crowd was deeply impressed. It seems this man was the police chief. He confessed to lying at some trial—said he made the whole thing up. Everything he said at the trial was a lie. Can you believe that? The police chief, no less."

The neighbor lady was shocked. "I don't think he can do that. It's against the law. You can't lie at a trial. You'll get in a heap of trouble. What trial was he talking about?"

"It was about a Lester trial. I suppose it was in Wabash," Mrs. Ellis answered.

"I think that's the name of the folks that live on the corner in the brick house. Their name is Lester. I remember because I stopped there to register them to vote when they moved. They had a son that was in trouble in Wabash, stealing or something. You say the chief lied about the whole thing. Can you beat that? I don't know what this world is coming to. I'm going to mosey down there and tell them. I bet they haven't heard about that. They might be interested in hearing that bit of news," the neighbor lady declared.

Later that morning, she and Thelma Lester had coffee and a sugar cookie in Thelma's kitchen, a bright spot overlooking the green lawn sloping down to the river. Thelma was shocked by the news she learned.

"A public confession in a church and the chief admitted lying at the trial? He put his hand on the Bible and took an oath. My God, what will happen to him now? He broke the ninth commandment—bearing false witness against your neighbor. God will punish him for sure, maybe strike him dead. He is going to need more than prayer. I wouldn't want to be in his shoes," Thelma said.

That night, Thelma Lester sent a telegram to Les Lang detailing the recent news about the Wabash Police Chief. Les had received the Pinkerton report suggesting Jerry Lester may not have been guilty. When his movie shoot was completed, Les opened the telegram and read it twice. The chief of police committed perjury? He was furious—this was too much! *The Pinkerton report and now this!*

"Get me my lawyer. Now!"

Les spoke briefly to his lawyer and then assembled a small group of his close advisors and explained to them the events at Wabash. They agreed it needed a heavy hand to shake them up. A judge in the group made a suggestion.

"Our friend, the California senator, has a son that is married to the daughter of the Indiana Lieutenant Governor. I think a message from Les to the son would result in a call to the lieutenant governor that would order the state attorney general to investigate the trial. That would scare the hell out of any local judge and prosecuting attorney. A phone call from Les Lang will get the job done."

The group agreed that was the route to take—start at the top—use your considerable influence to get the job done. The substantial funds they contributed to the senator over the years would move the plan along. Later that month, the Indiana Governor's office sent the state attorney general's office a "hurry up" request to investigate a trial that occurred in the Wabash County Circuit Court. The defendant's name was Jerry Lester, now deceased. The presiding court officer was Judge Terrance McCowen.

The Gun from Dooley's Desk

Chapter 16

TUESDAY MORNING, court clerk Bob Miller came to the judge's office and announced to all present some disturbing news. "Last evening, Fern called Zeno to come to supper. As he shuffled with his cane, he collapsed in the hall. Fern called Dr. Singer and caught him just as he was leaving the office. He came quickly, but Zeno was in a coma. He died of a massive heart attack. The body was taken to Johnson Funeral Home, and funeral arrangements will be announced later. The ladies of the Falls Avenue Church are assisting at the house."

Judge McCowen arrived a few minutes later and was informed of the latest news. His mind absorbed the facts quickly.

"This will have a major impact on any retrial attempt. The only remaining witness is dead. Yes, any retrial attempt is over." He felt relieved; a heavy load had been lifted.

Mayor Hutchens declared the city of Wabash would be in mourning for another police officer, the second in a year. He quickly appointed John Boyle, a veteran city policeman, as the new chief of police, making the announcement during the Monday evening city council meeting. The council approved unanimously. John was a local man, a Wabash High School football hero and a track star. He and his family were longtime loyal members of the Wabash Street Methodist Church.

He had served on the police force for several years, his wife worked at the local utility company, and his kids attended local schools. John possessed all the qualities needed for a new police chief. As the mayor pinned the gold chief's badge on John's suit coat, his family cheered, and the council members applauded. The city was back in good hands again. John Boyle was the salt of the earth.

. . .

Michael noted on the calendar that it was the birthday of Sam Jacobs, his college roommate, now a movie writer. He called him long distance to California. When they connected, Michael wished him a happy birthday, and each man described how his life was unfolding. Michael asked Sam how the script about the hobo trial was progressing.

"How soon will the movie shooting begin? I would like to schedule my vacation to come out and watch a movie being produced."

"Forget it. The hobo story is forgotten. Les Lang has started a major drama with three famous stars. This will be the biggest budget movie ever made. Watch for it in your neighborhood movie house. It will be a blockbuster," Sam replied. "Come out and visit anytime. We will find exciting things to do, but you will be disappointed watching a movie being filmed. It's as exciting as watching paint dry," he added.

. . .

Court clerk Bob Miller assembled a small group of officials in his office for a meeting: Judge McCowen, Prosecutor Plum, Mayor Hutchens, the chair of the county commissioners, and Lester's attorney, Joseph Sloop. The commissioner's office was represented, because in the case of a retrial, the county commission would be required allocate the necessary funds, something they were against.

Bob Miller opened the letter from the state attorney's office and read the contents aloud to the men assembled there. The letter asked the clerk to provide information pertaining to the trial and conviction of defendant Jerry Lester, which had occurred in the Wabash Circuit Court. This was an informal request to determine if further in-depth investigation should be performed.

"Please include any information obtained by the court since the trial that might have any consideration on a future retrial of the defendant." It was signed by State Attorney Jack Rolston.

The group determined this letter was the result of Chief Moore's public confession to committing perjury as it related to the trial. After much discussion, Attorney Plum responded.

"I suggest we instruct the clerk's office to respond in a very narrow scope. This is what I suggest." Plum stood up, folded his arms in front of his chest and leaned against the wall. After a moment to gather his thoughts, he began.

The Gun from Dooley's Desk

"This trial was the result of a homicide committed in Wabash City, Wabash County, Indiana. The defendant was apprehended by police action. An alleged accomplice was never identified or apprehended. Witnesses placed Lester in the location of the homicide on the exact day. Lester dictated a two-page detailed confession, admitting his role in the crime, signed it, and two sworn police officers witnessed this signature. Lester later recanted this action, but no evidence was presented to bolster his claim or cast doubt on the confession.

"The evidence presented at the trial was the result of sworn testimony by two law officers under oath. That is powerful evidence, legally obtained and duly admitted to the court. Nothing except the defendant's verbal denial of the confession was presented to disparage that evidence. The court's officers had no reason to doubt the veracity of the presented evidence, then or now. There has been no admissible evidence presented to court authorities by anyone that would cast doubt on the trial, the evidence, or the trial procedure.

"We must remember the words spoken by a very sick man months after the trial, under great stress, in an emotional setting are hearsay evidence, not given under oath, not even in a sound mind. We must not allow our court to be defamed by people who are not capable of determining what is legal evidence in court. We stand strong in our belief that the court acted in good faith, conformed to the Indiana State Law, and the jury's verdict was just and proper. Any events the defendant suffered after the trial are outside of this court's authority, and while we deplore the resulting death of Mr. Lester, this court is not in any way responsible.

"For your further information, please be informed, the police officers who witnessed the confession and testified are both deceased. The defendant Mr. Lester is deceased. These facts disclose the difficulty in obtaining testimony in a retrial situation. This describes the facts as they exist at present."

Clerk Bob Miller polled all in attendance, and all agreed the response was true and correct. The clerk's office would prepare an answer as described. The clerk and the judge would both sign as the Wabash Circuit Court Officers. The letter was promptly written, recorded and mailed to the state attorney's office.

Later, as State Attorney Jack Rolston read the answer to his inquiry to the Wabash Court, his mind raced. *Why is the governor's office so interested in a trial at Wabash, Indiana about some hobo and a failed robbery-murder? We are having a major crime wave in this state, and I must spend my time on this crap. Who is this guy Lester? Why is this so important? Who is pulling the chain that reaches into the governor's office? I smell something like money, and I don't like it. No sir, not one damn bit. I'm not going to proceed with flimsy evidence from a tent show by some preacher—a woman at that. What the hell do they expect from me, a damn miracle? They can take this retrial crap and shove it! I don't want any part of it!*

He carefully composed the answer that would stop any further attempts to pressure his office for a retrial. His response to the governor's office was a brief official letter.

Lieutenant Governor
State of Indiana
This office has determined after careful examination that there is no new admissible evidence that would alter the Wabash Circuit Court's decision in the State of Indiana Against Jerry Lester, nor were any court procedures violated. There is no new material to warrant a retrial, now or in the future. Our review concludes the court's decision stands unchallenged. This office regards the case as closed.
Jack Rolston
State Attorney

The letter was sent to the governor's office with a copy to the Wabash Court clerk's office.

Court clerk Bob Miller came to the judge's office carrying a letter and wearing a big smile. As he and Judge McCowen sipped black coffee, he read the letter from the state attorney concerning any retrial in the Lester case.

The clerk explained, "Jack Rolston's office is not in favor of any retrial. This apparently ends the push for a retrial from the governor's office. When the state attorney's office says it will not proceed, it's hard to see any further action. It's over and done. But I wonder who the big stick is that stirred the pot in secret. It had to be from a high spot to reach the governor's office."

The judge reflected a moment. "Yes, it's over. But it's a damn shame the first capital trial in thirty years had to be clouded by doubt because a couple of police officers decided to take it upon themselves to create evidence. Our court was duped and manipulated, and we didn't see through the scheme. It cast a cloud that will remain forever. I say it's a damn shame. But you are right. Jack Rolston is a tough cookie, and if Rolston's office says no, then it's all over and done. As for who stirred the pot, I say it goes straight to Hollywood, but we'll never know. My mother had an old Irish saying, 'If three people know, it's not a secret.'"

It was several days before the letter arrived at the lieutenant governor's office. After some time there, an assistant passed it to the proper person who relayed it to Les Lang. Les had expected some action to be taken, some new information to be developed, but no—nothing— total disregard of the facts. He was not just disappointed, he was unhappy, and now he was mad. Going through the political chain had not worked. *What will get the attention needed to bring this to the front? A movie—yes—a movie will get the entire country's attention. Damn bunch of hicks back in Wabash running the place. Well, look out! A new movie will tell the world what a bunch of crooks you are. You will be sorry you messed with Les Lang…*

Les picked up the phone, called the creative production office and gave them the order. "Set up a meeting with my top writers. The hobo story is back on track—big time—maybe a major hit to come. We are on a tear!"

The meeting was delayed two days until the complete writing staff could be present. Sam and several others were finishing up movies still in the shooting stage. They had to be available for script changes. Les wanted the group to feel the same compulsion that he felt. He took charge of the meeting and laid out his requirements. He listed his thoughts about the script as follows:

"The courtroom will be depicted as a low-key place, not very modern, with brass spittoons by every desk, the windows propped open and a lazy ceiling fan churning the air. There will be all wooden furniture, straight chairs, and wooden pews for the spectators. I see bare wooden floors, dark wainscoting with bare plaster above. A flag and a framed copy of the Constitution are the total decorations. It should be depicted as very "backwoods style," not too clean, not very modern.

"The judge is to look like a dull, below average guy that got himself elected even though he probably was not qualified. The clerk is an ordinary fellow, not capable of running a court, dressed in a white shirt and black suspenders. The prosecutor is to be a slovenly character. He chews tobacco, spits in the spittoon by his desk, is a sloppy dresser and slouches in court in his vest and rumpled white shirt with black tie. He clearly has the goal of convicting the defendant even if it requires false testimony or evidence. He dominates the court, and the judge allows it.

"The chief of police is a mean, ill-tempered character. At home, he is strict and quick to slap around the wife or kids. As a policeman, he is a person to be feared, quick to use the black-jack in his back pocket. His mode of operation was to beat them up then throw them in jail. His assistant is a dull-witted, large younger fellow, eager to follow the chief, not very capable, has a job and wants to keep it. He will do whatever the chief orders. They both will lie in court after swearing on the Bible to tell the truth. They want to convict this poor young defendant—and they do.

"The defendant is depicted as an average young unemployed man from a good family. His mom sings in the church choir. He is poor, has no steady job, works odd jobs and rides the rails from town to town. He has no training or skills for any trade, just manual labor. The depression has made him do things he normally would not do, but it caused him to get in trouble with the law. He could be one of a million young men caught up in the trials of the depression. His name is legion.

"Now you get the picture. Write me a script that will electrify the movie patron. Make him feel compassion for the poor downtrodden unemployed young men in this country. Make them feel this could be their son suffering from the evils of power hungry men in authority causing unfair convictions in courts all over the country. Bring it in close. This could be their son or the neighbor's son, unfairly convicted by men determined to show how powerful they are. We need to cast the spotlight of righteousness on these wicked men and bring them to justice. Justice will prevail—even in the backwoods of our nation."

Les now changed from the visionary to the authority figure. He stood up, walked around the room muttering to himself, and then quickly whirled to face the writers. "OK? Do we all get the storyline? Now get the ball rolling. This is a big budget project, and we expect it to be our major production this year. Sam, you lead this story. Get some talent aboard, get cracking on this project. Are there any questions? No? Then get to it! I expect a meeting in two weeks with a project report and preliminary storyline. I want to keep this moving at a rapid pace. This is a big money film—a major hit for this studio."

With those words, he left the room. The remaining writers got the message loud and clear.

"We are to create a story that transforms a local small-town bum into a national hero. We have to do it all on the silver screen, in budget and limited to ninety-five minutes story time. It must provoke millions of average citizens to swarm to the movie house and pay hard earned cash for tickets to see this 'must see' social epic. Holy crap! We are going to need divine help on this project," Sam declared.

Chapter 17

WHEN SAM GOT HOME that evening, he checked the mailbox, and there was a letter from home in his mom's handwriting. He felt a little guilty as he took the letter out. He could not remember if he answered her letter of last week. Mom and Dad were so proud of him working for a major Hollywood studio; they told all the friends back home in Delphi.

When Sam's mom was at the store, she encountered his high school English teacher Miss Rice. She was excited to hear Sam was employed as a writer in Hollywood. She had been convinced Sam would be lucky to graduate from high school. He needed to work harder and kid around less to get a passing grade from her. Sam was free-spirited and not too inclined to work very hard at anything. But four years at Indiana University transformed Sam into a dedicated writer willing and able to tackle any writing job.

In college, he worked two jobs: a bus-boy dishwasher at the Main Street Grill and stocking shelves at the Downtown Food Market. He learned writing for money was better than washing dishes—a painful learning experience. His parents were glad he had a good job. They just wished it was not so far away. They didn't get to see him very often.

The Gun from Dooley's Desk

But today, her letter was about them and the city of Delphi. This was the year of the Delphi Centennial. Delphi was created at the end of the Indian Wars. The last battle was fought at Prophetstown, just a few miles away. Chief Tecumseh's Indian army was defeated by General Wayne in 1812, and as part of the settlement, a large parcel of land north of the Wabash River and west of Tippecanoe River was deeded to the Indians. The settlement was established, and a trading post and a grist mill were built for the Indians. It became the town of Delphi.

In later years, it was the western lock of the Erie Canal. Many settlers passed through the town on the way to settle the rich Kankakee prairie land. The city was planning a three-day celebration including a pageant put on in the town's Main Street. All locals would be in 1830s costume. Men would grow beards, and a contest for the best beard began. A replica of an 1836 canal boat as used on the canal was being built as a parade float, and old muskets were procured from attics and barns to be used by the replica army unit. Sam's mom was riding on a float and demonstrating how to churn butter. Dad, sporting a new beard, would be on a float that depicted the farming tools used at that time. They were excited about being part of the parade.

She asked Sam if he could make a trip home for the celebration. He had not been home in a long time. He answered right away. Yes, he would be there and wouldn't miss it for the world. Sam sent a letter to his friend Michael, informing him about the trip to Delphi and that this would be a fine opportunity for them to get together for a visit. Michael agreed. He was looking forward to seeing his college roommate again. A good time would be had by all.

Sam and Michael watched the Delphi parade, visited all the exhibits, sampled all the food at the different tents, drank beer at the Old Time Tavern and had their picture taken by the local newspaper, the Delphi Daily. The family and friends ate supper at the Canal Corner Restaurant. As Sam listened to the conversations around him, he remembered these were real folks in a real world discussing real problems. He realized how Hollywood was a false world, and he was getting caught up in the fake life of Tinseltown. His Midwest values were being tested.

Sam visited Michael in Wabash and met Lucille, soon to be his wife. Together they visited the house on West Hill Street. The house was being repaired and repainted for their future home. They drove to Erie Point and met Lydia and John. The next day, they went for a swim then to lunch at the Elks Club. Michael knew everyone in the clubroom and introduced Sam to all. As they were filling their plates, Michael saw the judge enter. He invited him to join them and introduced Sam to his uncle.

"Sam, meet my Uncle Terrance McCowen."

Sam shook hands and warmly greeted him. He instantly liked the tall Irishman. After they sat down, Michael related about how he and Sam lived together while in college. Now Sam was working in Hollywood as a writer for a major studio.

"I have learned it's a damn sight better than washing dishes," Sam added. They kidded about how life treats

The Gun from Dooley's Desk

different people. Sam asked Terrance what he did in Wabash.

"I am the Circuit Court Judge of Wabash County."

Sam nearly fainted—he quickly asked, "Did you preside at a trial for a man named Jerry Lester?"

"Yes, that trial was held in my court, and I presided. I am surprised the news of that trial would be of interest in Hollywood, California."

"After lunch, can we go someplace and talk privately? It is very important," Sam asked.

"How about my office at the courthouse, it's just a short walk from here."

Later that afternoon in the judge's office, Sam explained his orders from Les Lang. The judge called in clerk Bob Miller to hear the story, and Bob suggested they call Frank Plum as he was also part of the trial. Frank came up, met Sam and settled in to hear what this was all about. Sam explained in some detail what was planned in the movie script, how they were to be portrayed, how the story would claim Lester was convicted by false testimony and lying witnesses.

"A Pinkerton detective, hired by Les Lang, has written a report that cast doubt on the trial and conviction of Lester. Now Lang has received word that the chief of police made a public confession before a hundred people that his testimony was a lie. The movie as planned by Les is to depict the court and all the officers as a bunch of lying hicks, out to convict an innocent young man just because he was poor and unemployed."

Sam was distraught. He explained he was part of a plan to destroy these people, to slant the truth to gain the fickle public's attention and sell movie tickets. Sam wondered if all this could happen just by putting words on paper. He told them his moral code was being tested, and he was very uncomfortable.

The people listening to the story were dismayed. They were not like that. They were just ordinary folks doing their jobs, and they were amazed anyone would depict them as crooks and liars, eager to convict an innocent man. Who would believe such a story?

Michael listened quietly; he was the only person in the room that had knowledge of Coleman's confession to this crime in the suicide note. *What should I say—or do?* For the moment he said nothing.

• • •

That evening, Sam shared the story with his parents. They were shocked such a thing could happen—lives destroyed by a movie that is twisted and slanted against ordinary Midwest folks just like them.

"Sam, sometimes you have to do the right thing. You know what is right. This story you tell is not right. Do you want to make a living destroying people that were doing their jobs as best they can?" Sam's mom asked.

"This can be a big event for you if you play it right. Offer a different but better story. Make Les think this is his production, his dream. You can do that, just have a plan. Good luck," his dad added.

Sam delayed returning to Hollywood. He sat by the gentle, flowing Tippecanoe River, watching the leaves slowly drift by, clearing his thoughts and making plans.

The Gun from Dooley's Desk

Friday afternoon, he caught the Wabash Cannonball train headed west to St. Louis. His plan was taking shape. He watched the farms and towns drift by, and the click, click of the tracks lulled him into a restful slumber. After dinner, the porter made up his berth, and Sam rested and finalized his plan.

The next morning in St Louis, he caught the City of Los Angeles, a new streamline train, the latest thing on tracks—yes Sam traveled well. Sam had planned his conference with Les Lang carefully, so he could present his plan in a manner that Les would like. He fell asleep in his compartment, confident he had it right. Sam arrived in Los Angeles Union station, took the PE streetcar to his street and walked home, happy to be there.

The next morning, he had trouble starting his car; it had sat for two weeks. When he arrived at the studio, he saw the yellow Cord convertible parked in Les' reserved parking space and knew the man was there. It was now up to him to sell the story. He asked the receptionist to get him a closed-door meeting with Les as soon as possible. He would need about an hour of his undivided attention. Then he went to his office to wait.

Instead, he looked up and there was Les standing at his desk. Les was in a jovial mood.

"Hey kid, glad you are back. It worries me when I come in here, and your desk is empty. I hope you brought back some of those great apples from the Delphi orchard. They are the sweetest apples in the world! Now, what the hell do you want to see me about?"

Sam closed the door, pulled up a chair next to his boss and began his story. "Les, I have been out in the Midwest this past two weeks, visiting with the very folks you want to buy tickets to your movies. I want to tell you the mood has changed. The public is convinced big business is out to cheat them. They resent the glory pictures of Hollywood stars standing by big expensive cars in mink coats in the summer. They want to go back to the old days when life was not so demanding when each family took care of their own and when honesty and values were important and had meaning.

"The hobo depression era is what they are now experiencing. They don't want to spend good money to buy a ticket to see the misery they see every day on the streets of their home town. No, they want to escape the harsh dark reality. They want to buy a ticket to make them feel better. Life is hard now, hopefully in time it will get better. They yearn for a ticket to spend two hours viewing this country's good times.

"Think about it, the greatest story of America is the Old West when men could control their lives, when the Colt six-gun made all men equal. Families moved west, took all their possessions, built farms, ranches, towns, and cities. They overcame obstacles: the Indians, the desert's dry weather, the barren land, the long distances. They prevailed over great odds, and by the grace of God, they were successful. Ranches, railroads, cities, and towns grew to become the core of America. Les, that's the story. The public will pay hard earned money to see the great building of America by the common man."

Les pushed a button on his phone. "Get us coffee and some of those donuts!" He stood, walked around the desk

The Gun from Dooley's Desk

and sat down again, staring intently at Sam. The coffee and donuts arrived, and Sam continued.

"I see the story unfold; it's 1855. A young man named Lucas Lang travels by steamboat from Louisville down the Ohio and down the Mississippi to Leavenworth, Kansas Territory. He is headed west, not sure where but west. He thinks he will travel to Dodge City. He has heard things about Dodge. At the dock, he meets a man just returned from Dodge City going east, who needs to sell his horse and saddle to get the fare to go back home.

"Lucas studies the horse, a good firm chestnut horse, good coat, good teeth, and good hooves. But when he sees the saddle, he is really impressed! It is a black, hand-tooled Mexican saddle with silver conchos, hammered silver buckle ends, and silver corner plates. This is not a working saddle. This is a show saddle, and Lucas knows he can't afford it. He has only $400.00 to get him across Kansas to Dodge City. No, Lucas can't afford the horse and saddle, but he sure wants it. He imagined how good he would look in that saddle on that beautiful horse.

"The northbound boat is coming in two days; he has some time to think about the deal. He hears the man offer the horse and saddle to others but most want to take the stage west, not ride a horse across Kansas. The man has no takers on the morning the boat arrives. Lucas offers him $250.00—the man is insulted.

'You cheap bastard, the saddle is worth more than that!' he shouts.

"Now, the northbound boat is at the dock, loading freight and passengers. Soon it will sail, the captain wanting to get past the shoals before night. The man returns to Lucas, asks for a fair offer on the horse and saddle. He must sell it now or load it on the boat. Lucas plays it tight; he offers the man $200.00.

'That's it—no more—take it or leave it!'

"The man curses and cries out about being cheated, but in the end, he accepts the four $50.00 gold pieces. He writes out a receipt to Lucas for the horse and saddle. Lucas can only write his name; he cannot read. He doesn't want the others to know he can't read, so he just puts it in his pocket.

"The next day he sets out for Dodge City with a group riding in that direction. There is safety in numbers. Kansas Territory is a dangerous place, so they travel together. At night, when they stop for supper, all the men admire the hand tooled, silver mounted Mexican saddle. Lucas is very proud—a good horse plus a magnificent saddle. It takes two weeks to get to Dodge City, a hard ride over bad trails and poor roads. When they arrive, they are surprised to find two men hanging from the gallows in the town square. There had been a shooting, leaving three men dead several days before. The local sheriff caught two men, the local magistrate ordered them hanged, and the sheriff carried out the gruesome order. Frontier justice at its worst!

"Outraged citizens have gone to Fort Dodge to convince the U.S. Marshal and the Federal Territory Judge to come to town and arrest the local sheriff and the magistrate for murder. They have no authority to order the men hanged. They are self-appointed city officials. Lucas takes a room at the Dodge City Inn and boards the horse at the livery stable. He asks around town whether

The Gun from Dooley's Desk

he should ride south to Texas for a job herding cattle north to the Railroad Line in upper Kansas. That would be about a three-month job ending before winter. Or, should he go west to the Denver area where there have been rich silver mines established. That job would last all year round.

"The next morning, after breakfast at the Inn, he is crossing the street when he is attacked by two men. They claimed they are sheriff's deputies and are arresting him. They take him to the sheriff, who questions him if he owns that chestnut horse with the Mexican saddle. Lucas replies he bought them in Leavenworth for $200.00, that he has a paper and produces the receipt. The sheriff, who possibly can't read, declares it bogus—no good. He says he recognizes the saddle as one stolen months ago, the owner shot, and the horse and saddle disappeared. The sheriff will take the horse and saddle as evidence, and he charges Lucas as a horse thief—a very serious charge.

"That afternoon the magistrate orders a trial. The sheriff testifies the horse and saddle were stolen and the owner shot. Lucas says he had a receipt, but the sheriff took it and now it's lost. He has no evidence proving him innocent. The magistrate finds Lucas guilty and orders him hanged in the town square the next day at sundown. He is locked in the jail until then. The Sheriff moves the horse and saddle to the stall behind the jail—he owns them now. He will not permit any horse thieves in Dodge City!

"The next day before noon, the stage from Fort Dodge arrives, carrying the U.S. Marshal with two well-armed deputies, the Federal Territory Judge, and his clerk.

The marshal goes directly to the sheriff's office, arrests the sheriff and locks him in his own jail. Lucas is the only other prisoner, and the marshal asks Lucas why he's in there. Lucas tells him about the false arrest, the ten-minute trial, and the false horse thief conviction. The sheriff destroyed the receipt to convict him. He is innocent, charged and convicted by a crooked sheriff that wants the horse and saddle for himself. They plan to hang him to hide the evidence.

"The marshal releases Lucas and suggests Dodge is not a safe place for him to stay. The marshal tells Lucas he has arrested the sheriff and is delivering him to Fort Dodge to stand trial for murder. The sheriff has some friends that would not like that turn of events, and there might be trouble.

'This is Dodge City, and trouble happens every day. Get out of Dodge and don't come back. You are in danger here!' the marshal orders Lucas. Lucas sells the horse and saddle to the liveryman for five $50.00 gold pieces. He gets a job as an assistant driver and armed guard on the Overland Stage Coach Line, headed to Denver the next morning. When the stage pulls out of Dodge, Lucas is up on the seat with the driver. He is glad to be leaving Dodge City; he came close to being buzzard bait there."

Les took a sip of coffee, then walked over to his bar and poured himself a brandy. He looked at Sam. "Want some brandy?"

"No, thank you," Sam replied.

"So, what happens next?"

"This is the storyline. Six frontier men and one buxom lady in her best dress and bonnet are riding in the

The Gun from Dooley's Desk

Overland Stage Coach Line from Dodge City, Kansas to Denver, Colorado, over rough roads and stage trails. Each has a special reason to go to Denver—each has a special reason to hide from their past—each has the spirit to win. They demonstrate that when the stage is stopped by outlaws in Kansas and attacked by Indians in the grasslands. Both times, the passengers fight back, driving off the attackers. Each man carries a six-gun even the lady has a two-shot Derringer in her purse, and the driver has a young man Lucas to help drive the team of horses. He rides outside up on the driver's bench, has a 30-30 Winchester rifle and a spare revolver under the seat. He wears a Colt in his holster.

"When the stage is stopped by outlaws in Kansas, Lucas whips out the Colt and shoots two desperados; the others turn and run. In the grasslands, a small Indian party of braves wanted to raid the coach, but Lucas uses the Winchester 30-30 to great advantage. With deadly aim, he drops several Indians, stopping the attack. Les, he is not a hobo, he is a young adventurer heading west, not knowing what awaits him in Denver. He is the same young man as Jerry Lester in Wabash. This could be your relative, named Lucas Lang. I see him as an agile young man with many good qualities, seeking adventure—you would be proud of him." Sam took a sip of coffee and continued.

"Les, this is the story. Let's do it big, film it on location in Colorado with several big-name stars and think about this. Let's do it in Technicolor. This movie will be the biggest thing out of Hollywood this season. A major studio producing a big Western, using several big-name stars, filmed on location in the desert and mountains, all in spectacular Technicolor.

"Let's name it 'STAGE WEST,' produced and directed by Les Lang, America's number one cowboy. Let me head up the writers, and we will give you a script that all America will pay to see. We know westerns draw patrons. A big western in color with famous stars will draw thousands of ticket buyers. It will make you the most famous studio in the country. No other studio is planning a major western.

"We will have the premiere at Grumman's Chinese Theater on Hollywood Blvd. The black limousines will arrive with the stars and other big shots. You will arrive riding your white horse in your white western cowboy attire, fancy boots, two silver six-guns in your holsters and a big white hat. The press will love it when you have that white horse rear up with you waving that white hat to the crowd.

"Every paper in the country will carry a front-page picture of Les Lang opening the premier of "Stage West" in Hollywood. Pathé News will feature it on Saturday in every movie house in the country. Remember, movie patrons are looking for a movie that makes them feel good, proud to be an American. Nothing is more American than the western cowboy. Les, this is your movie, and the public awaits your colossal production. Here is your opportunity to make movie history now."

Sam paused, took a deep breath and then cautiously asked, "Well, what do you think of it?"

"Damn, I need to send you writers out east every year, so you can find a good story. Yes, I like everything about it. I need to see if I have a great female under contract for the stagecoach role. Yes, Technicolor is great, but you know what that costs. It's a damn arm and leg but worth it for a spectacular movie. 'Stage West.' That's good! We will ask the legal team if it is available. Lucas Lang, we will research that name, see if it's OK." Les paused to catch his breath.

"How about we shorten it to Luke Lang? That fits the western image better. The promotional guys can contact both Colt and Winchester and see if they would each produce a special gun marked 'STAGE WEST.' They could sell a bunch of them—we get a cut of course. If we had the premiere in Denver instead of Hollywood, would it be more authentic?

"There are always those damn bankers to contend with. I'll have the art department make up some storyboards that will visually dramatize the story when I have the bankers over to see the idea of the movie. One will be Luke shooting off the masked desperados that are attempting to hold up the stage, the other passengers with their six-guns drawn and ready to fight back. Another depicting the Indians attacking and the passengers shooting their guns. Luke, up in the driver's seat, fires his 30-30 Winchester rifle with deadly results.

"A third Indian brave, dressed only in a loin cloth, is looking inside the coach at the lady, eager to get her. She has her pearl handled, two shot Derringer in her hand and shoots. His horse rears and he falls off the horse at a gallop. Oh, yes—this will be a real story, real action, and real drama. It will be a new western story, a spectacular display of action, location, and talent.

"Yes, I see many possibilities. I like it. Damn, you sure came back from Indiana with a head full of great ideas. The home cooking or the weather must be good for you. Remind me to send you home next year to refresh your mind and body."

As Les left the room, he mused, *Wow, imagine me on my white horse prancing up Hollywood Boulevard and arriving at Grumman's Theater, the press and thousands of fans watching. That's a real scene stealer. I like that! I'll have to train that white stallion not to be spooked by camera flashbulbs. Holy cow, would Pathé News carry it nationwide? This is a great idea! I love it!*

The Gun from Dooley's Desk

Chapter 18

LUCILLE AND HER MOTHER were very close. They shared secrets and celebrated joys and sorrows together. That spring evening, when Lucille confided she and Michael were having discussions about marriage, her mother was swept up with joy. A very bright young man with a college degree and a career with the new state police was a good catch for her daughter. He seemed to be a very polite, well-mannered man—even though he was Irish. She wondered about her future grandchildren. They would have an Irish name; would that make them Irish or what. She would need to pray about that. She reasoned that God would make it all work out.

    Sarah immediately pictured the wedding in her mind—she would be in charge. It would be held in the Presbyterian church. She could see it all now: the church smothered in flowers, candle holders on the pews lining the aisle, a white runner down the center aisle, that special arch covered in flowing white flowers. Oh, the beauty of it all! The wedding party all in formal dress, gowns for the ladies, black tux for the men. The bride's dress would be directly from L.S. Ayres top floor wedding designers. The two ladies would travel to Indianapolis and stay at the Claypool Hotel for several days while the dress is fitted. She visualized it all now; she and Lucille having lunch at the Ayres Tea Room, then shopping together in Indiana's finest department store.

The groom would be in a well fitted black tux as would be the best man. She paused and wondered who that might be. *If he's from Erie Point, will he have a tux? Oh well, we can rent one at the Beitman & Wolf Store in Wabash.* The bridesmaid would wear a light pink gown from L.S. Ayers. Sarah pictured herself in a gown from that elegant department, Mother of the Bride Shop.

The minister would wear a white robe with gold trim, the choir in the new special light blue robes trimmed in white and gold braid. Mr. Galen would perform on the large pipe organ. The music would be stunning as he was a master musician. *How thrilling is the thought of it all!* Naturally, the reception would be held at the Women's Club, very formal. *We will hire a band out of Chicago for dancing. It will be the talk of the town.* She would see the society editor at the paper gets all the information, make sure the photos are featured. She wondered aloud, "Should I plan for about a hundred for dinner?"

Michael attempted to visit his parents often, and during one visit he confided to his mom that he and Lucille were discussing marriage. He told it in a matter of fact way, just that they were "thinking" about a wedding in the future.

Immediately, Lydia's mind sprang into action. The wedding—she would be in charge. The marriage would be held in the Erie Point Catholic Church, Father Gibbons presiding. She could picture how the church would look, flowers everywhere; the bridal flowers would be a cascading hand-held bouquet. The choir dressed in white robes with Kelly green trim would sing selected Irish wedding hymns accompanied by the church organ. Michael's friend Terry O'Brien, a beautiful Irish tenor, would sing at the church and during the reception at the grand Masonic Lodge Assembly Hall. *Are there enough chairs in the hall to seat everyone?*

Michael would wear a white tux. *Who will be the best man? Perhaps a friend from the state police.* The new black Packard sedan would be used to carry the wedding party to the reception. She would hire the Huntington College Dance Band to play at the reception, "swing" was their specialty. *What a great day it will be! I must develop the menu. Should I plan for about a hundred people?*

• • •

The wedding of Sarah King Coleman and Oliver Pezzell was Wabash's social event of the year. It was held at the Women's Club in the formal garden, a perfect location for the couple to exchange their vows. Due to the cooler weather, the gardens were at their prime. Reverend Warner conducted the ceremony, the couple exchanged vows, and the groom slipped a large diamond ring on Sarah's finger.

The dinner and reception were held in the formal ballroom, and everyone agreed it was a beautiful wedding. The piano was played, Barry Tyner sang the wedding song, and the guests cheered. The dinner and champagne toasts brought joy and happiness to all. The band performed, and the guests danced. It was a great social

The Gun from Dooley's Desk

event in the depression, and every little bit of joy was appreciated.

Their honeymoon to the Wisconsin Dells was a perfect start to their wedded life. Sarah moved into the West Hill Street home that Oliver had been remodeling and improving the past year. It was a beautiful showplace home for Wabash's newest important couple. Oliver and Sarah were at the top of the Wabash society and business community.

The same painters and carpenters that had worked at the Pezzell home now worked daily at the Coleman home, getting it ready for the next couple to make their new life there. Sanding and refinishing the oak hardwood floors and the large oak stairway was a massive job. New linoleum was laid on the kitchen floor, a new Roper gas range and a new Norge refrigerator were installed. Fashionable green and white striped awnings were added to the west windows to reduce the sun's heat in the rooms.

The telephone line was extended upstairs, so a phone could be answered easily on either floor. The Stewart Painting Company carefully painted the entire house inside and out and restored it to the showplace condition it once was. The garage received the newest invention, two overhead doors—the first in town. This West Hill Street house would be the future home of Lucille and Michael McCaffery when they started their married life together.

Chapter 19

PRESIDENT RICHARD PRESTON called the monthly meeting of the board of directors of the City Bank to order. The secretary read the minutes, and the board worked through the old and the new business in an orderly manner. Oliver Pezzell attended to make a report on the status of the Coleman company and its ability to make the next payment toward the large mortgage. The meeting was routine until the item of unfinished business came up. There was an unexpected issue.

Mr. Finney, the bank bookkeeper, had a problem. He held up an invoice in his hand for the annual insurance policy premium covering the Coleman factory loan. The face amount of the policy was for $500,000.00 on the life of Mr. Coleman, now deceased. In the past years, the premium was paid by the bank and then reimbursed by the Coleman account. The policy was owned by the bank. The beneficiary was the bank first, and any remaining funds after the loan was retired would go to the Coleman heirs. The policy excluded Mrs. Coleman; she had a substantial wealth of her own.

The loan balance had been reduced to $260,540.00. Mr. Coleman was deceased; the bank needed to collect the funds and pay off the loan.

The Gun from Dooley's Desk

"What should I do? Who is responsible for collecting this policy? The face amount will clear the banknote. How do we handle the balance to the Coleman family?" Mr. Finney asked.

Director Erwin quickly spoke up and made a suggestion. "Here is an opportunity to make some money for the bank. Why are we paying the Coleman family anything? What the hell, Sarah Coleman has more money than she will ever spend. Isn't there some way to keep that extra cash? No one outside this boardroom knows about that guarantee Life Insurance Policy. We purchased it years ago. I had just been appointed to the board. I remember, Coleman had to get a physical for the policy. I doubt he told anyone we made him buy a policy to cover the loan. Why can't the bank just keep the extra money? It will sure help offset some of the big losses we have now."

Another director added, "We should think about this before we pay the Colemans anything. We own the policy, and it was used to guarantee the loan. I think we should make the decision on who gets the money. It is our policy, so it's our money. Why can't the bank just keep it? *No one will ever know.*"

The president responded angrily. "Because it is not legal, that's why! We may have big problems as a bank, but we are sure as hell not going to steal from our customers, not while I'm holding the gavel. I discussed this with the bank attorney. His opinion is the insurance company will write the checks when we send a death certificate and the payoff number. The contract is very clear; we will get our mortgage satisfaction money, and the residue goes to the Coleman heir. Frank Plum's law firm has handled the legal affairs for the Coleman and King family for years. They will know how to direct the heir's funds to the proper account. If there is any tax problem, our bank accountant will handle it. Now I think this issue is resolved legally and the matter closed."

Richard Preston rapped the gavel and looked at the men sitting around the table.

"We have completed the order of business; this meeting is adjourned. Thank you for attending."

Oliver Pezzell sat there amazed! He just heard two bank directors propose to defraud the Coleman heir of her insurance money. They appeared to be willing to commit outright theft by deception. *What has the depression mindset done to these bank directors? This little bit of information may be helpful in the future.* He tucked it into his memory. One thing for sure, he would be damn careful when dealing with this bank from now on.

. . .

The court office clerk brought in the day's mail. One letter addressed to the judge from the United States Government commanded attention. The judge opened the envelope and withdrew the letter. It was from a man he met at a forum held concerning the new government programs being brought on by the Roosevelt Administration. They had been seated together several times during the two-day session. The Supreme Court in 1935 had revoked the American Agricultural Agency (AAA), the backbone of the Federal Farm Reconstruction

Program. New replacement programs were being developed within the guidelines of the Supreme Court to restart American agriculture, a critical issue to the farm belt in Indiana and the Midwest states.

This letter was from an assistant administrator named Gordon Pence. He was requesting assistance as the new Rural Electrification Program was to be established in this district. He needed recommendations of qualified people to serve on the local board. They would need a local manager and several employees. Because many farmers were afraid of the government coming onto their property, the office would need an attorney with local connections to draw up easements for the wire lines and access across farm property. Farmers were a special lot. They liked the idea of having electric service; they could have a radio in the house and a light in the barn. But they didn't want to shake hands with the government to get it.

In the following days, the judge wrote down several names including the former president of the Farmers Bank for the board, and for the manager, the young man employed by the city water plant. He was a Purdue graduate electrical engineer and was scratching out a living as an electrician. He had extensive construction experience from working at the Chicago World's Fair in 1933. McCowen suggested the Law Office of Plum & Plum, well connected for a hundred years in the county and very knowledgeable about local farm real estate. Before sending the letter, he had lunch with Frank and asked if the firm would like to have some government work.

"Anything would be good right now; business is very slow. What kind of work? Frank asked.

The judge thought it would be mostly easements, property leases, abstracting, and some contracts. Perhaps there would be some appraisals, the same work they had done for years. Frank was pleased with the idea of having business with steady payment.

"That would be great," he answered. "Let's go for it."

The judge mailed the letter and after some time forgot about the request. One day, a white 1935 Plymouth two-door with a red and black REA emblem on the door parked in front of the Plum office. The gentleman introduced himself as the area agent for the new REA Program in the county. When he was seated at Frank's desk, he outlined the program the government had designed for the county. Frank was amazed—this was much larger than anyone had thought. The total expenditure would be more than twenty-five thousand dollars with over five thousand to be spent the first year. Every service would require contracts, easements, legal descriptions, and leases. Frank was impressed at the amount of work involved, and he was surprised at the level of details. Government work demanded pages of details.

The agent offered the work to the Frank Plum's law firm because the Circuit Court Judge Terrance McCowen recommend them. The district director was a friend of the judge, had a great regard for his local knowledge and respected his recommendations. Frank eagerly accepted the offer and set up his younger brother and a former abstract worker for the REA work. It soon became a

The Gun from Dooley's Desk

beehive of activity. An additional typist was hired to complete the pages of contracts. Frank was very pleased with the additional business for the firm; it also gave his kid brother a chance to get some great experience working in the land use business. The Law Office of Plum & Plum took on a new look of activity, and the additional cash flow was greatly appreciated.

One evening, Frank and three friends were playing pool at the Elks. One of the players asked Frank, "Are you going to run for judge in the coming election?

"No, I am going to run for re-election as prosecutor. We have a good judge right now. He runs a good court, and I think he should be re-elected," Frank answered.

The Republican County Chairman was sitting in a chair watching the pool game and heard the remark. He was astounded! He had planned on Frank heading the Republican ticket in the coming election as their candidate for circuit court judge. He expected to win back the court and end this blot on county politics forever. *Now Frank admits this damn Democratic judge is doing a good job! What the hell is this?* He was very disturbed by this news; it reflected on his ability to keep the county elected officials entirely Republican. *How could Frank do this to the Republican Party?*

He spoke out. "What the hell is happening to our party, our country, and this county? My God, it's bad enough we have that bastard Roosevelt in the White House and a damn Democratic governor. Now we have an Irish judge in our courthouse. Those damned Democrats are taking over everywhere. Soon they will control everything, maybe even running things here in Wabash! It's not going to be the same ever again."

Chapter 20

THE WABASH PRESBYTERIAN Church survived the depression better than most local churches. Their members were more affluent, very loyal to the church and they loved their minister Reverend Warner.

The American Home Missionary Program was supported by the Presbyterian church. Their missionaries would visit cities around the United States and speak or perform at local churches. The Wabash church was very active, bringing in visiting speakers, missionaries, and musical groups to educate and entertain the congregation.

One interesting program was an Irish born Presbyterian Minister, a lady named Pastor Makemie. She lived and ministered to the poverty-stricken Indians living in the Arizona and New Mexico deserts. She traveled part of the year to raise money to help these American Indian tribes survive in the harsh environment and depression times. The rest of the year, she was their pastor, living and surviving with them. She was one of the best-known missionaries in America at that time, and she was scheduled to speak at the Wabash Presbyterian Church about her Indian Ministry.

Sarah and Lucille planned to attend the afternoon program at the church. Sarah asked Lucille to invite Michael and Lydia and see if they would enjoy hearing the

The Gun from Dooley's Desk

Irish Missionary. They readily accepted the invitation, and all attended the program. This gave Sarah and Lydia an opportunity to become better acquainted. Lydia was impressed with the size and beauty of the church but was surprised there were no kneeling pads in the pews. *If they don't kneel, what do they do at church? Just sit there? This is strange.*

Pastor Makemie proved to be an exciting speaker, a Presbyterian preacher with an Irish dialect. She received offering money for the Indians and enjoyed a healthy applause from the attendees. Lydia and Pastor Makemie visited and discovered their ancestors were from near-by counties in Old Ireland.

"It is a small world," the Pastor declared. "Ireland and Arizona have a lot in common."

The four went to the Coleman home to visit and enjoy a cup of tea before Michael and Lydia returned to Erie Point. As they progressed through the house, Lydia felt a familiar sense of dread. Terrible memories of Coleman's advances put her in a state of turmoil. *He still controls me today! No! I won't let him! He's gone, and I'm in control of me now!*

She quickly excused herself to powder her nose and retreated to compose herself. After a few minutes, she felt recovered enough to join the others. Soon, the two ladies were discussing the coming marriage and the challenge of blending the two families and the two churches. One issue to be resolved was the problem of the bride's escort. What male figure would walk her down the aisle that day? She had no living father or brothers, but after careful negotiations, it was determined her new step-father would do the honors. Oliver had a distinguished appearance, a manner of authority, and besides, Lucille adored him.

Other issues were not so easily settled. The thought of the wedding in Erie Point was outside Sarah's ability to stomach. This event was so important it had to occur as she envisioned, in her church with her minister and her wedding plan. "Our family has been part of that church for over fifty years; it's our heritage." She added, "My gracious, we could not change it now, that's out of the question!" She flushed at the thought.

Lydia was dismayed anyone could consider the wedding anyplace but the church in Erie Point. She remarked firmly, "For the past one hundred years that's where our family gets married. It would be a sin to change it now! Our family's history for generations has been linked to that lovely old church, to change now would tear our birthright to shreds." She shuddered at the thought of such an occurrence. It was beyond her ability to comprehend, and she felt threatened by the suggestion.

The back and forth was growing heated, their voices rising but concealing the stress behind the conversations between the mothers. Michael was uneasy, but he was wise enough to keep quiet—these three women were the most powerful women in his world right now. Not one mortal man could reason with them. Even Solomon might be stressed to find the right solution. Lucille was embarrassed, and she was determined to settle this issue quickly on a positive note. She used the same plan she used every day in school with her fifth graders.

The struggle ended abruptly when Lucille suddenly stood up with a look on her face that meant she was not going to put up with any more disagreement. "Stop this bickering! You two better reach a complete agreement about every detail of this wedding in the next two weeks or Michael and I will just elope! We mean it. We will have Michael's Uncle Terrance marry us in the courtroom. He can do that you know—it's quite legal. I'm sure there have been many marriages performed there, so it is not anything new. Now you have two weeks—you can do it—just work together. That's it," she said firmly, her face flushed with annoyance.

The two mothers instantly got the message. The next two weeks were a beehive of activity. There were several lunches at the Women's Club and many long telephone conversations, but at last, the plan was finalized. In the process of give and take, a strong relationship developed between the two women. Each appreciated the strengths and commitment of the other. They were very different in birth and background, but in many ways, they were cut from the same cloth.

• • •

As the wedding plans progressed, one detail that needed to be completed was the blood test. Indiana law required a couple to get a blood test and the physician to sign off that they did not carry a disease. Michael and Lucille wanted to go to Huntington, so that Lucille could meet his favorite Aunt Phyllis and Dr. Nagle at the doctor's new office. After meeting the couple, Dr. Nagle performed the necessary blood tests. When he completed the tests, Phyllis filled out the state forms. It was all good-natured banter until she asked Lucille to list her birth parents' names.

"I don't know my actual birth parents; I was adopted as an infant. My parents legally adopted and raised me. My mother used to joke that I was left with the milk delivery."

Phyllis responded, "OK, I will just list their names. Legally adoptive parents will be fine; it's just a form for the state."

"My adoptive parents are Garl and Sarah Coleman, West Hill Street, Wabash, Indiana. My father is deceased," Lucille said.

Phyllis was astonished by that response! She paused to gain her composure. "Please repeat that. I didn't get that exactly."

Lucille repeated the Coleman name and address. Phyllis finished the form, signed and stamped her RN seal on it and handed it to Michael. She turned to Lucille and gave her a hug and a big smile. "Congratulations on your coming marriage, you two make a lovely couple."

After the couple departed, Phyllis was shocked by this extraordinary turn of events! She was very alarmed. *How could this situation happen? What will this mean? Should I tell someone, should I do something? My God, why me? Of all the girls in the world, how did Michael get engaged to this one, the baby girl we left in a basket on Coleman's doorstep years ago?* She recalled the night. They both had been so confident. *No one will ever know.* Now the events of twenty-four years ago were coming back to haunt them.

Michael and Lucille drove back to Wabash, and as they arrived at the steel bridge in the village of Markle, they stopped at a little pull off to look at the peaceful river

The Gun from Dooley's Desk

wandering through the small town. It was a beautiful view, and they took some time to relax and absorb some of nature's splendor. Lucille took some pictures with her new Brownie Kodak camera.

"I heard you tell Aunt Phyllis your mother said you were delivered with the milk. Is that really true?" Michael asked casually.

Lucille laughed. "Oh yes, in fact, Mom used to sing a little ditty when I was a child. It goes, 'The milkman delivered milk by the light of day—the angels left my basket in the very same way.' Later as I was growing up, our neighbor Mrs. Turner used to babysit me when Mom went to the store. She told me of my arrival in a basket. I thought all babies came in a basket until I got older. After I started school, I don't remember it being mentioned; it just wasn't important. I can't see why anyone would be interested now, my God, it's been twenty some years ago."

Michael absorbed that bit of information, then he gently inquired, "I heard you tell Aunt Phyllis you don't know your birth parents. Is that a fact?"

"That's true. I've only known Mom and Dad Coleman—that's all I need—that's all I want to know. After you and I are married, we will be a new family. I will leave my parents and cleave to my husband, just as the Bible says."

Michael reflected for a moment, watching the water work its way around a log stuck in the bend. "Yes, you are right, it was a long time ago. I think the less said about this the better. It happened over twenty years ago, and it's not for local gossip. Yes, the whole thing should be forgotten."

But Michael's mind was afire. Now, the complete story was unfolding, and he could see it clearly. His Aunt Linda as a teenager being sexually molested by Garl Coleman, resulting in a baby, Lucille, his intended bride-to-be. This explained Coleman's need to murder Russell after he discovered the baby was the teenage secret of Linda, now the judge's wife. Russell's intention was to blackmail the judge, exposing his wife's secret to the world, a despicable plan. Garl Coleman's death, his suicide note confessing his role as the shooter, Aunt Phyllis' involvement in protecting her husband, and his mom stealing the gun from Dooley's. My God! This was all a well-kept secret these many years until Russell dug up the dirt, intending to use it for a wicked purpose.

Russell was an evil man. *The genie is out of the bottle now, but how do we put it back?* His mind reeled, and an old saying came to mind. "What a tangled web we weave when first we practice to deceive." He tried to remember where he learned that phrase. Was it from the Bible or senior English class? His mind was full. He could not remember where he learned it, but it was certainly true. He was living it.

The Gun from Dooley's Desk

Chapter 21

THE WEDDING WAS HELD in the century-old church, the largest wedding ever held at Erie Point. The church was filled with all the Erie Point families, dressed in their finest Sunday clothes along with the cream of Wabash business and society. Gary Temple, Michael's friend from college, came up from Cincinnati to play the organ. The church altar was decorated with large floral arrangements of white gladiolus, lilies, roses, and mums all designed by the best florist in Wabash. The candelabra were embellished with matching white flowers and flickered, giving a soft glow to the beautiful stately church.

The members of the choir wore their new white robes with the Kelly green angel embroidery, their sweet voices filling every corner of the church. When the sound of Terry O'Brien's rich Irish tenor rang out, the church was completely silent. Few of the guests had ever experienced such a tenor voice. He sang the wedding song, and when he finished, there was not a dry eye in the entire congregation.

The bride wore a white lace gown with a hand embroidered bodice and matching pearls on her chapel-length train. She carried a long cascading bouquet of specially ordered gardenias, rosebuds, and stephanotis with delicate trailing ivy. Her veil of illusion flowed behind her as she walked proudly down the aisle holding the arm of her step-father Oliver. Lucille's eyes twinkled when she saw her beloved Michael standing at the end of the aisle waiting for her. He was so handsome in his white tux, rented from Beitman & Wolf for this most special occasion. The uniformed Indiana State Police Officers lined the walkway. Their blue and gray uniforms brought added dignity to the event. Father Gibbons performed the ceremony making sure the wedding was conducted in the true Irish tradition. Sarah Coleman was proud of the event and didn't even faint!

Lydia was impressed the Wabash Newspaper sent a photographer to the church. The pop of the flash-bulbs both before and after the ceremony recorded the event. The picture of the happy couple as they exited the row of state police officers was featured on the social page of the paper the following day. The social editor wrote a three-column article about the wedding including quotes and pictures of both Sarah and Lydia. The new Packard was used to transport the wedding party to the reception in Wabash. The weather was perfect for enjoying the lavish reception.

A huge white tent had been erected in the side yard of the Elks Lodge. A dance floor was installed along with two bars. Chef Randy and his staff served a sit-down dinner for one hundred guests. Eddie Allen and his six-piece orchestra provided music for dancing. After several hours with their guests, the couple retired to change for their honeymoon trip. They would travel from Wabash in Ike Bailey's private train car directly to Niagara Falls, Mr.

Bailey's wedding gift to the couple. Only the best for this special couple!

Later, as the train glided over the tracks, they enjoyed the luxury of the private car. The click, click, click of the rails offered a relaxing time after the strenuous day. Lucille noticed a small basket with a green bow on the table. She looked inside and discovered some unique small wedding gifts, both from Aunt Phyllis. Michael's was in a small cloth sack. He removed the item, an elk's tooth with a band of gold and an eyelet to wear it on a neck chain or a fob. Michael smiled and said he would wear it to the lodge meetings.

Lucille opened her special gift and discovered it was a small fine Irish handkerchief, with Kelly green embroidery of a baby in a basket. Lucille exclaimed, "How nice! That's me, the baby in the basket. I'll bet Phyllis made this for me. I love her so. She is so sweet. She sure seemed surprised when I told her about my arrival in a basket at the Coleman's that summer morning. I guess that doesn't happen very often."

Michael smiled. "Yes, I am quite sure she was surprised, and no, there are new laws that keep that from happening now." His mind recalled the chaos that one baby brought. *Thank God, it doesn't happen anymore.*

The Niagara Falls honeymoon was a six-day event; then the train car was returned to Wabash and parked on the Allen Street siding. Ike Bailey was there with his big Buick sedan to carry the newlyweds to their West Hill Street home. The suitcases and the shopping bag of Niagara Falls souvenirs were packed carefully in the trunk. Ike cheerfully delivered the couple to the newly painted and remodeled home. They unloaded it all on the new front porch and remarked how beautiful the house appeared. The porch had a new floor, a new porch swing, and chairs with lovely covers. There was a new front door and a substantial screen door. The house was completely painted. It was so fresh and beautiful; they were all impressed. On the new wall mailbox was a polished brass nameplate, "The McCaffery's," announcing the new occupants of the house to the world.

The couple thanked Ike for his wonderful gift of the private train car to Niagara Falls for their honeymoon. It was an experience they would cherish forever. Ike wished them well and departed. They stood on the front porch as Michael unlocked the new polished brass lock on the front door. He swung the door open and turned to his bride with a big Irish smile. "Am I going to get to carry you over the threshold into our new home?"

Lucille laughed and jumped up into Michael's strong arms. She kidded him. "I didn't realize you are such a man of tradition, but this is great! Yes, carry me inside, I'll love it."

He carried her across and carefully put her down after they were inside the gleaming new home. Michael pretended to be serious as he greeted her and said, "Welcome home, Mrs. McCaffery."

She laughed and gave him a big smile as she recalled, "I have been carried through that door twice in my life, first as a baby in a basket, now as a bride by my handsome Irish husband. Today is the best time of my life—it can't get any better than this as we start our life together. I love you, John Michael McCaffery, and I always will!"

Chapter 22

MORNING MEETINGS at the City Bank were unusual, but the directors had a big problem. That's why all directors, all officers, major stockholders, and the bank attorney were gathered around the large mahogany conference table in close attention. The bank auditor was explaining the requirements of the Federal Government's new BANK ACT of 1935 and what it would mean to City Bank. The bottom line was that much of the reserve funds now used by the bank would be classified as "below requirements" or "not investment quality." City Bank was not broke, just lacking the depth of deposits and cash on hand for daily business. The bank needed a substantial influx of new investors' cash, but that wasn't going to happen in the depression.

One possible solution was to purchase Farmers Bank down the street and merge their assets and depositor's cash together. Later Farmers would be allowed to go under after City had stripped out the necessary business to keep the bank alive. The owners of Farmers agreed; they would be rewarded in the sale. Farmers was a state-chartered bank owned by a local family with no extra money to back up their weak bank. They would be happy to get rid of a headache in exchange for some cash and some stock in City Bank.

The Gun from Dooley's Desk

What was the problem? The bank needed approval from the new Federal Bank Agency, a regulatory agency set up by the Roosevelt Administration in each state to oversee local banks. City Bank's President Richard Preston had contacted the agency's director with this merger request, but it was declined. The group discussed the problem at length. A decision was to find someone with some knowledge to work with the new agency and get the needed approval. Otherwise, the City Bank could not meet the new financial requirements to stay in business. The future for City Bank was grim—its existence was in doubt.

After the meeting adjourned, Frank Plum and Dick Preston stopped by the Elks for lunch, a corned beef sandwich and a cold beer. They had just sat down when Judge McCowen walked in for his lunch. They waved and invited him to join them.

The judge sat down and asked, "Well gentlemen, what's new in the banking world?"

"Most of the new government regulations are tough to understand, difficult to administer and impossible to follow. Banks have enough trouble without some new government agency in Washington writing volumes of new rules," Dick Preston replied.

The judge laughed. "Remember, the government is putting people to work, mostly writing regulations no one understands and laws no one can obey. But they have put people to work. That seems to be the Washington way. God help us," he said

"You're right, Judge. The guy we need to help us won't even answer our letters. I don't know who the hell put this guy Hurlock in charge of our banking world," Dick Preston added.

"You better get ready for regulations; they are coming out of Washington fast and furious. Believe me, new laws are flowing out like water. I don't know who will be able to keep up with all of them. You say your guy's name is Hurlock? That's an unusual name. While in college, I worked one summer at the state fairgrounds with a guy named Hurlock. We painted bleachers that summer. I think we made twenty cents per hour working in the hot sun. He was a student at Anderson, studying finance. The only finance *we* had was the twenty cents an hour or nothing if it rained. I remember one week it rained three days, and we lived on a loaf of bread and a can of Spam that week. Hurlock you say, I haven't heard from him in years. I wonder what he's doing now."

The three men finished their lunch, told several stories and enjoyed a good time together.

Frank noticed the moisture running down the sides of the beer glasses, pooling at the bottom on the table top. He held up his glass and said to his friends, "Buying that refrigerated cooler for the beer was the best improvement this club has made in years."

They all agreed it had been a good thing to do and resulted in great tasting beer. As Frank and Dick departed, they shook the judge's hand and wished him well.

"I'll look up my old painting buddy Hurlock. It probably won't be your guy, but with a strange name like Hurlock, you never know. Sometimes it's a small world."

Two weeks later, the judge called Frank and Dick to meet him for lunch at the Elks. When they met and were seated at their table, the judge smiled and handed Dick a letter. It was addressed to Mr. Bruce Hurlock, Director, Federal Finance Agency, Indianapolis, Indiana.

> Dear Bruce,
> This letter will introduce my good friends, City Bank President Richard Preston and Attorney Frank Plum to you. They are men of highest integrity and are my special Lodge brothers. Please offer them your help and guidance with their bank merger problem. All assistance will be appreciated by your old painting buddy.
> Speaking to you on the phone brought back many memories of the good and bad times we had together. When you visit Wabash to announce the bank merger, we will reminisce about those days. It was interesting to learn you are also an Elks member. We will have lunch there; it is a really friendly place. Again, I add, you have my personal thanks for your assistance to my friends, and I am looking forward to seeing you again.
> Sincerely,
> Terrance McCowen
> Judge, Wabash Circuit Court.

When he finished the letter, Dick was overcome with emotion. "I don't know how to thank you; this is the key to saving the bank. What can I say? This is beyond my wildest dream," he stammered. "Our combined boards appreciate what you have done, and we certainly will be attentive to any requests you may have in the future. Again, I add my sincere personal thanks. It was great of you to do this for us."

"What great news! This merger will save our bank. Thanks to you, we will wind up with one strong bank for the county, and City Bank will serve this county for years. Now there is new hope. It will be tough, but we will survive this damn depression," Frank added

Frank's opinion of the judge had reached a new high. He leaned back in his chair with his fingers laced behind his head, and his heart swelled as he reflected on recent events. *Damn, think of all that has happened, all because we didn't want any Irishmen in our club. We certainly judged that one wrong. My God just think about it. Garl and John are gone, and four other people died. How could they have been so wrong about this guy? He is really an honorable man and a great friend. We were wrong in our judgment of him. I am so happy he is one of us now.*

The End

About the Author

Rex Sims was born in the Midwest during the depression of schoolteacher parents. He married his high school sweetheart, joined the Marine Corps, raised two kids and succeeded in business. Rex always had a flair for writing short stories and speeches but waited until he finished an active business career before attempting a novel.

His working career involved designing, engineering and fabricating huge components for the pollution control industry, metal contracting and air control dampers.

Rex's hobbies include bass fishing, cart racing, old cars, and gun collecting. For years, he loved to fly his plane to favorite fishing spots from Texas to Canada.

Now Rex resides on the sunny Florida Gulf Coast with his wife Peggy, overseeing several small businesses and properties. The kids are close by. Steve is a successful realtor, and Susie is president and manager of the family florist business, a 32-year-old enterprise.

Latest endeavor: Rex and son-in-law Jim conceived the idea to open an ice cream shop, and now Jim manages the most popular spot in Historic Bonita Springs.

Contact Information

To contact J. Rex Sims, please email:

jrexsims@gmail.com

This novel and the Kindle version are available at www.amazon.com.

Made in the USA
Columbia, SC
02 July 2018